"I'm going to kiss you."

It was a warning and a plea all wrapped up in one.

"Mazie," J.B. whispered.

She put a hand behind his head and pulled him closer. "Yes."

He was trembling, almost out of control. Yet they had barely begun.

She arched into his embrace, melding their bodies from shoulders to hips. The look in her eyes was his undoing: part yearning, part caution. She didn't completely trust him.

"I've pictured you like this in my head," he groaned. "But I never thought it would happen."

She nipped his bottom lip with sharp teeth. "And why is that? I thought the larger-than-life J.B. Vaughan was irresistible to the female sex."

"You're sassy. And no, I'm not irresistible. You aren't even sure you like me. And you sure as hell don't trust me."

The flicker of her gold-tipped eyelashes told him he had hit a nerve.

But her voice when she answered was steady. "Apparently it's possible for me to crave someone... even if he's a bad boy with a terrible reputation."

* * *

Blame It On Christmas is part of the Southern Secrets series from Janice Maynard.

Dear Reader,

I love holiday books. December makes me think of hot chocolate and roaring fires and sleigh bells. Of course, Christmas in the South can sometimes be more shorts and flip-flops than reindeer sweaters and woolly socks.

If you live on the coast (far enough south), you may not have a white Christmas, but the spirit of the holiday burns just as brightly.

I really like writing friends-to-lovers books. A hero and heroine who already have a past together (whatever that might be) can find lots of sparks along the way when they connect later in life. Whether they were childhood playmates or high school sweethearts or even old enemies, the tale lends itself to drama and high-stakes passion.

So sit back, enjoy your favorite hot beverage and cheer for love and the season of peace and goodwill for all.

Happy reading!

Janice Maynard

JANICE MAYNARD

—

BLAME IT ON CHRISTMAS

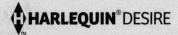

Recycling programs
for this product may
not exist in your area.

ISBN-13: 978-1-335-97193-7

Blame It On Christmas

Copyright © 2018 by Janice Maynard

Printed in U.S.A.

USA TODAY bestselling author **Janice Maynard** loved books and writing even as a child. After multiple rejections, she finally sold her first manuscript! Since then, she has written fifty-plus books and novellas. Janice lives in Tennessee with her husband, Charles. They love hiking, traveling and family time. You can connect with Janice at www.janicemaynard.com, www.Twitter.com/janicemaynard, www.Facebook.com/janicemaynardreaderpage, and www.Instagram.com/janicemaynard.

Books by Janice Maynard

Harlequin Desire

The Kavanaghs of Silver Glen

A Not-So-Innocent Seduction
Baby for Keeps
Christmas in the Billionaire's Bed
Twins on the Way
Second Chance with the Billionaire
How to Sleep with the Boss
For Baby's Sake

Highland Heroes

His Heir, Her Secret
On Temporary Terms

Southern Secrets

Blame It On Christmas

Visit her Author Profile page at Harlequin.com, or janicemaynard.com, for more titles.

This book is for every guy or girl who has found the courage to ask someone out and then been shot down. It hurts. But true love finds a way. 🙂

One

"The answer is no!"

Mazie Tarleton ended the call, wishing she had a good old-fashioned receiver she could slam down on a cradle. Cutting off a phone conversation with the tap of a red button wasn't nearly as satisfying.

Behind her, Gina—her best friend and coworker—ate the last bite of her cinnamon crunch bagel and wiped cream cheese from her fingers. "Who's got you all riled up?"

The two women were in Mazie's office, a cramped space behind the elegant showroom that drew tourists and locals to All That Glitters, Mazie's upscale jewelry store in Charleston's historic business district.

Mazie dropped into a chair and scowled. "It's J.B.'s real estate agent again. He's making her badger me."

"You mean J.B. who wants to offer you a ridiculous

amount of money for this building that's falling down around our ears?"

"Whose side are you on anyway?" Mazie and Gina had met as freshmen at Savannah's College of Art and Design. Gina was aware of Mazie's long-standing feud with Charleston's highly eligible and incredibly sexy billionaire businessman.

Gina flicked a crumb from her cashmere-covered bosom. "We have dry rot in the attic. A heating system that dates back to the Civil War. And do I need to mention that our hurricane policy rates are set to triple when the renewal is due? I know you Tarleton people are richer than God, but that doesn't mean we should thumb our noses at a great offer."

"If it were anybody but J.B.," Mazie muttered, feeling the noose of inevitability tighten around her neck.

J.B. Jackson Beauregard Vaughan. The man she loved to hate. J.B. Vaughan had been on her personal hit list since she was sixteen years old. She loathed him. And she wanted to hurt him as much as he had hurt her.

"What did he ever do to you?" Gina asked. Her perplexed frown was understandable. J.B. Vaughan was the prototype for tall, dark and handsome. Cocky grin. Brilliant blue eyes. Strong features. And shoulders that were about a million miles wide.

"It's complicated," Mazie muttered, feeling her face heat. Even now, the memories were humiliating.

Mazie couldn't remember a time when J.B. hadn't been part of her life. Way back when, she had even loved him. As an almost-brother. But when her hormones started raging and she began seeing J.B. in a whole new light, a spring formal at her all-girls prep school had presented itself as the perfect opportunity to do some very grown-up experimentation.

Not sex. Oh, no. Not that. She was aware, even then, that J.B. was the kind of guy who *knew things*, and she wasn't ready to go down that road.

She called him on a Wednesday afternoon in April. With her nerves humming and her stomach flopping, she blurted out her invitation.

J.B. had been oddly noncommittal. And then, barely four hours later, he had showed up on her doorstep.

Her father had been locked in his study with a nightcap. Both Jonathan and Hartley, her brothers, had been out on the town doing something or other.

Mazie had answered the front door.

Because she felt weird about inviting J.B. inside—though he'd been there a hundred times before—she stepped out onto the wide veranda and smiled at him tentatively.

"Hey, J.B.," she said. *"I didn't expect to see you today."*

He leaned against a post, his posture the epitome of cool, high school masculinity. In a few weeks he would be eighteen. A legal adult. Her heart beat faster.

"I wanted to talk to you face-to-face," he said. *"It was nice of you to ask me to the dance."*

"Nice?"

It seemed an odd choice of words, especially coming from J.B.

He nodded. "I'm flattered."

Her stomach curled defensively. "You didn't actually give me an answer on the phone," she said. *Suddenly, her hands were ice, and she was shaking all over.*

J.B. shifted from one foot to the other. "You're a cute girl, Mazie. I'm glad you're my friend."

He really didn't have to say anything else. She was smart and perceptive and able to read between the lines. But she'd be damned if she'd let him off so easily. "What are you trying to say, J.B.?"

Now a dark scowl erased some of his cocky charm, but none of his brooding sexuality. "Damn it, Mazie. I can't go to that dance with you. You shouldn't have asked me. You're little more than a baby."

Her heart shriveled. "I'm not a child," she said quietly. "I'm only a year younger than you are."

"Almost two."

The real surprise was that he had kept track. Because of the way their birthdays fell on the calendar, he was right. She took three steps toward him. Inside, she was falling apart. But she wouldn't let him see what he was doing to her self-esteem. "Don't make excuses, J.B. If you won't go out with me, please have the guts to say so."

He cursed vehemently. With both hands, he scraped his slightly-too-long blue-black hair from his face. "You're like a sister to me," he said.

The words were muttered, barely audible. In fact, he spoke them in the direction of the floor. A less-convincing lie would have been hard to find. Why was he throwing up walls between them?

Mazie was breathing so rapidly she was in danger of hyperventilating. Clearly she had misread the situation. J.B. hadn't come here tonight because he was fond of her, or because he wanted to see her.

He was standing on her front porch because he was

too much of a Southern gentleman to say no to her over the phone.

A nicer person might have made the situation easier for him. Mazie was tired of being nice. She slipped her arms around his waist and rested her cheek on his broad chest. He was wearing a navy T-shirt and faded jeans with old leather deck shoes. Decades ago, he would have been a classic James Dean. Bad boy. Rule breaker.

When she touched him, his entire body went rigid. Nothing moved. Except one thing. One startling and rather large thing.

Jackson Beauregard Vaughan was aroused. Since Mazie had plastered herself against his front, it was rather impossible for him to hide. She found his mouth with hers and threw every ounce of her undiluted teenage passion into an eager, desperate kiss.

J.B. tasted wonderful, exactly like he did in her dreams, only better.

For a moment, she thought she had won.

His arms tightened around her. His mouth crushed hers. His tongue thrust between her lips and stroked the inside of her mouth. Her legs lost feeling. She clung to his shoulders. "J.B.," she whispered. "Oh, J.B."

Her words shocked him out of whatever spell he'd been under. He jerked away so hard and so fast, she stumbled.

J.B. never even held out a hand to keep her from falling.

He stared at her, his features shadowed in the unflattering yellowish glare of the porch light. The sun had gone down, and the dark night was alive with the smells and sounds of spring.

Very deliberately, he wiped a hand across his mouth. "Like I said, Mazie. You're a kid. Which means you need to stick to the kiddie pool."

His harsh words, particularly coming on the heels of that kiss, confused her. "Why are you being so mean?" she whispered.

She saw the muscles in his throat work.

"Why are you being so naive and clueless?"

Hot tears sprang to her eyes. She wouldn't let them fall. "I think we're done here. Do me a favor, J.B. If you ever find yourself in the midst of an apocalypse—zombie or otherwise—and if you and I are the only two humans left on the planet, go screw yourself."

"Mazie…hello… Mazie."

Gina's voice shocked Mazie back to the present. "Sorry," she said. "I was thinking about something."

"About J.B., right? You were ready to tell me why you loathe the man after all these years, and why you won't sell this property to him, even though he's offered you three times what it's worth."

Mazie swallowed, shaking off the past. "He broke my heart when we were teenagers, and he was kind of a jerk about it, so yeah… I don't want to hand him everything he wants."

"You're being illogical."

"Maybe so."

"Forget the money. Hasn't he also offered you two other properties that are prime locations for our shop? And he's willing to do a trade, easy peasy? What are you waiting for, Mazie?"

"I want him to squirm."

J.B. had bought up every single square foot of property in a two-block strip near the Battery. He planned a massive renovation, working, of course, within the parameters of historic Charleston's preservation guidelines. The street-level storefronts would be glitzy retail space, charming and Southern and unique. Upstairs, J.B.'s vision included luxurious condos and apartments, some with views of the picturesque harbor and Fort Sumter in the distance.

The only thing standing in J.B.'s way was Mazie. And Mazie's property. And the fact that he didn't own it.

Gina waved a hand in front of Mazie's face. "Stop spacing out. I understand wanting to torment your teenage nemesis, but are you seriously going to stonewall the man just to make a point?"

Mazie ground her teeth until her head ached. "I don't know if I'm willing to sell to him. I need time to think about it."

"What if the agent doesn't call you back?"

"She will. J.B. never gives up. It's one of his best qualities and one of his most annoying."

"I hope you're right."

J.B. slid into the dark booth and lifted a hand to summon a server. He'd worn a sport coat and a tie for an earlier meeting. Now, he loosened his collar and dispensed with the neckwear.

Jonathan Tarleton was already sitting in the opposite corner nursing a sparkling water with lime. J.B. lifted an eyebrow in concern. "You look like hell. What's wrong?"

His friend grimaced. "It's these bloody headaches."

"You need to see a doctor."

"I have."

"Then you need to see a better one."

"Can we please stop talking about my health? I'm thirty, not eighty."

"Fine." J.B. wanted to pursue the issue, but Jonathan was clearly not interested. J.B. sat back with a sigh, nursing his beer. "Your sister is driving me crazy. Will you talk to her?" He couldn't admit the real reason he needed help. He and Mazie were oil and water. She hated him, and J.B. had tried for years to tell himself he didn't care.

The truth was far murkier.

"Mazie is stubborn," Jonathan said.

"It's a Tarleton trait, isn't it?"

"You're one to talk."

"I've literally put my entire project on hold, because she's jerking me around."

Jonathan tried unsuccessfully to hide a smile. "My sister is not fond of you, J.B."

"Yeah, tell me something I don't know. Mazie refuses to talk about selling. What am I supposed to do?"

"Sweeten the pot?"

"With what? She doesn't want my money."

"I don't know. I've always wondered what you did to piss her off. Why is my little sister the only woman in Charleston who's immune to the famous J.B. Vaughan charm?"

J.B. ground his jaw. "Who knows?" he lied. "I don't have time to play games, though. I need to break ground by the middle of January to stay on schedule."

"She likes pralines."

Jonathan drawled the three words with a straight

face, but J.B. knew when he was being taunted. "You're suggesting I buy her candy?"

"Candy…flowers… I don't know. My sibling is a complicated woman. Smart as hell with a wicked sense of humor, but she has a dark side, too. She'll make you work for this, J.B. You might as well be prepared to crawl."

J.B. took a swig of his drink and tried not to think about Mazie at all. Everything about her flipped his switches. But he couldn't go there. Ever.

He choked and set down his glass until he could catch his breath.

Hell's bells.

The Tarleton progeny were beautiful people, all of them. Though J.B. barely remembered Jonathan's poor mother, what he recalled was a stunning, gorgeous woman with a perpetually sad air about her.

Jonathan and Hartley had inherited their mother's olive complexion, dark brown eyes and chestnut hair. Mazie had the Tarleton coloring, too, but her skin was fairer, and her eyes were more gold than brown. Amber, actually.

Though her brother kept his hair cut short to tame its tendency to curl, Mazie wore hers shoulder length. In the heat and humidity of summer, she kept it up in a ponytail. But during winter, she left it down. He hadn't seen her in several months. Sometimes J.B. dropped by the Tarletons' home on Thanksgiving weekend, but this year, he'd been tied up with other commitments.

Now it was December.

"I'll take the candy under advisement," he said.

Jonathan grimaced. "I'll see what I can do," he conceded. "But don't count on any help from me.

Sometimes if I make a suggestion, she does the exact opposite. It's been that way since we were kids."

"Because she was always trying to keep up with you and Hartley, and you both treated her like a baby."

"I suppose we could have been nicer to her. It wasn't easy growing up in our house, especially once Mom was gone. Poor Mazie didn't have any female role models at all."

J.B. hesitated. "You know I would never do anything to hurt her business."

"Of course I know that. Don't be an ass. Your wanting to buy her property makes perfect sense. I can't help it if she's being deliberately obstructive. God knows why."

J.B. knew why. Or at least he had a fairly good idea. One kiss had haunted him for years, no matter how hard he tried not to remember.

"I'll keep trying. Let me know if anything works on your end."

"I'll give it my best shot. But don't hold your breath."

Two

Mazie loved Charleston during the holidays. The gracious old city was at her best in December. The sun was shining, the humidity occasionally dipped below 60 percent, and fragrant greenery adorned every balustrade and balcony in town. Tiny white lights. Red velvet bows. Even the horse-drawn carriages sported red-and-green-plaid finery.

She'd be the first to admit that summer in South Carolina could be daunting. During July and August, tourists had been known to duck into her shop for no other reason than to escape the sweltering heat.

She couldn't blame them. Besides, it was the perfect opportunity to chat people up and perhaps sell them a gold charm bracelet. Or if they were on a tight budget, one of Gina's silver bangles set with semiprecious stones.

Summer was definitely high season. Summer brought an influx of cash. The foot traffic in All That Glitters was steady from Memorial Day until at least mid-October. After that it began to dwindle.

Even so, Mazie loved the holiday season best of all.

It was funny, really. Her own experience growing up had certainly never been a storybook affair. No kids in matching pajamas sipping cocoa while mom and dad read to them in front of the fire. Despite the Tarleton money, which provided a physically secure environment, her parents were difficult people.

But she didn't care. From Thanksgiving weekend until New Year's Day, she basked in the season of goodwill.

Unfortunately, J.B.'s sins were too heinous to include him on Santa's good list. Mazie still wanted to find a way to make him suffer without putting her own business in danger.

When the real estate agent called the following day with another offer from J.B., Mazie didn't say no.

Not immediately.

Instead, she listened to the Realtor's impassioned pitch. When the woman paused to catch her breath, Mazie responded in a well-modulated, exceptionally pleasant tone of voice. "Please," she said politely, "tell Mr. Vaughan that if he is hell-bent on buying my property, perhaps he should come here and talk it over with me in person. Those are my terms."

Then once again, she hung up the phone.

This time, Gina was polishing an enormous silver coffee service they kept in the front window.

She hopped down from the stepladder and capped

the jar of cleaner. "Well," she said. "You didn't hang up on her. I suppose that's progress."

Mazie frowned at a smudge on one of the large glass cases. "I thought I was nauseatingly nice."

"Most people think being nice is a good thing."

"True. But not always. We'll see what happens now. If J.B. wants this place, he's going to have to show his face."

Gina blanched and made a chopping motion with her hand.

Mazie frowned. "What's wrong with you?"

The other woman was so white her freckles stood out in relief. And her eyes bugged out of her head. She made a garbled noise.

When Gina continued her impersonation of a block of salt, Mazie turned around to see what was prompting her friend's odd behavior.

A gaggle of middle-aged women had entered the shop together. The tiny bell over the door tinkled, signaling their presence.

While Mazie and Gina were deep in conversation, J.B. Vaughan had slipped in amid the crowd of shoppers, topping the women by a good six inches.

"I think she's surprised to see *me*," he said. His smile was crooked, his gaze wary. "Hello, Mazie. It's been a while."

His voice rolled over her like warm honey. Why did he have to sound so damn sexy?

The man looked like a dream. He was wearing expensive jeans and a pair of even more expensive Italian leather dress shoes. His broad shoulders were showcased in an unstructured, raw linen sport coat that hung open over a pristine white T-shirt. The shirt was just tight enough to draw attention to his rock-hard abdomen.

Oh, lordy. She had demanded he come in person, but she hadn't realized what she was asking for.

She swallowed her shock and her confusion. "Hello, J.B." A quick glance at her watch told her there was no way he could have gotten there so quickly. Unless he had *already* decided to challenge her refusal to sell face-to-face. "Have you talked to your real estate agent this morning?"

J.B. frowned. "No. I just came from the gym. Is there a problem?"

Mazie swallowed. "No. No problem."

At that precise moment, J.B.'s phone rang.

Mazie would have bet a million dollars she knew who was on the other end of the line. Because she saw his expression change. A huge grin flashed across his face. The Realtor had just passed along Mazie's message.

Damn the man. *She* had wanted to call the shots… to *make* him come plead his case in person.

Instead, he had cut the ground from beneath her feet. J.B. had walked into her shop because it was *his* idea, not because he was toeing some imaginary line or meeting a challenge she had thrown down.

Her temper sparked and simmered. "What do you want, J.B.? I'm busy."

He lifted an eyebrow. "Cleaning a glass counter? Isn't that above your pay grade, Ms. Tarleton?"

"It's my shop. Everything that happens here is *my* business."

Gina squeezed past Mazie. "Excuse me," Gina muttered. "I need to check on our customers."

Mazie should have introduced her redheaded friend to J.B. The two of them might have met at some point in the past, though it was unlikely. But Gina seemed bent on escaping the emotionally charged confrontation.

J.B. held out a red cellophane bag. "These are for you, Mazie. I remember Jonathan saying how much you liked them."

She stared at the familiar logo. Then she frowned, sensing a trap. "You brought me pralines?"

"Yes, ma'am." His arm was still extended, gift in hand.

It might as well have been a snake. "You realize the shop is half a block from here. I can buy my own pralines, J.B."

His smile slipped. The blue irises went from calm to stormy. "A thank you might be nice. You weren't spanked enough as a kid, were you? Spoiled only daughter..."

She caught her breath. The barb hit without warning. "You know that's not true."

Contrition skittered across his face, followed by regret. "Ah, damn, Mazie. I'm sorry. You always bring out the worst in me." He grimaced and pressed the heel of his hand to his forehead. "The candy was a peace offering. Nothing sinister, I swear."

She grabbed the bag of pralines and set it on the counter behind her. She and J.B. were standing at the far back of the store in front of a case of men's signet rings. Hopefully, all of the current customers were shopping for themselves.

"Thank you for the candy." She straightened her shoulders. "Is that all?"

J.B. stared at her, incredulous. "Of course that's not

all. Do you really think I wander around Charleston dropping off candy to random women?"

Mazie lifted one shoulder. "Who knows what you do?"

Watching J.B. rein in his temper was actually kind of fun. It helped restore her equilibrium. She *enjoyed* getting the upper hand.

After a few tense moments of silence, he sighed. "I'd like to show you one of my properties over on Queen Street. You could double your square footage immediately, and the storage areas are clean and dry. Plus, there's a generously sized apartment upstairs if you ever decide to move out of Casa Tarleton."

The prospect of having her own apartment was tempting, but she and Jonathan hadn't been able to leave their father on his own. Stupid, really. He'd been a less-than-present parent, both emotionally and otherwise. Still, they felt responsible for him.

Over J.B.'s shoulder, Gina telegraphed her concern like a flamingo playing charades.

Mazie decided to play J.B.'s game. At least for a little while. What she really wanted was to make him think she was seriously considering his offer. And then shut him down. "Okay," she said. "I suppose it couldn't hurt to take a look."

J.B.'s reaction to her quiet statement was equal parts pole-axed and suspicious. "When?"

"Now is good."

"What about the shop?"

"They don't need me." It was true. Mazie was the owner and CEO. In addition to Gina, there were two full-time employees and three part-time ones, as well.

J.B. nodded brusquely. "Then let's get out of here. I'm parked in a loading zone."

"You go ahead. Text me the address. I'll be there in fifteen minutes. All I need to do is grab a coat and get my purse."

He frowned. "I can wait."

"I'd rather have my own car, J.B."

His eyes narrowed. He folded his arms across his chest. "Why?"

"Because I do, that's why. Are you afraid I won't come? I said I would, and I will. Don't make a big deal out of this."

He ground his jaw. She could almost see the hot angry words trembling on his lips. But he said nothing.

"What?" she whispered, still very much aware that they had an audience.

J.B. shook his head, his expression bleak. "Nothing, Mazie. Nothing at all." He reached in a pocket and extracted his cell phone, tapping out a text impatiently. "I sent you the address. I'll see you shortly."

J.B. should have been elated.

The first hurdle was behind him. He had finally convinced Mazie Tarleton to look at another location for her jewelry business. That was *huge*. And it was certainly more than his real estate agent had been able to accomplish in the last twelve weeks. Even so, his skin felt itchy. Being around Mazie was like juggling a grenade. Not only was she an unknown quantity, he was in danger of being sabotaged by his own uneasy attraction.

He was determined to keep his distance.

Nothing with Mazie was ever easy, so he paced

the sidewalk in front of the empty property on Queen Street, praying she would show up, but fearing she wouldn't.

When her cherry-red Mazda Miata turned the corner at the end of the street and headed in his direction, he felt a giant boulder roll from his shoulders. Thank the Lord. He was pretty sure Mazie wouldn't have come today unless she was ready to take him up on his offer.

She parallel parked with impressive ease and climbed out, locking her snazzy vehicle with one click of her key fob. He saw her, more often than not, in casual clothes. But today, Mazie was wearing a black pencil skirt with an ivory silk blouse that made her look every inch the wealthy heiress she was.

Her legs were long, maybe her best feature. She walked with confidence. In deference to the breezy afternoon, she wore a thigh-length black trench coat. To J.B. she seemed like a woman who could conquer the world.

As he watched, she tucked her car keys into her coat pocket and joined him. Shielding her eyes with one hand, she stared upward. He followed suit. Far above them, etched in sandstone, were the numerals 1-8-2-2, the year this building had been erected.

He answered her unspoken question. "The most recent tenant was an insurance firm. The building has been sitting empty for three months. If you think it will serve your purposes, I'll bring in an industrial cleaning crew, and we can get you moved with little to no interruption of your daily business."

"I'd like to see inside."

"Of course."

He'd made sure there was nothing to throw up any red flags. No musty odors. No peeling paint. In truth, the building was a gem. He might have kept it for himself if he hadn't so badly needed a carrot to entice Mazie.

For years he had tried to make up for his youthful mistakes. Becoming a respected member of the Charleston business community was important to him. The fact that he had to deal with Mazie and a very inconvenient attraction that wouldn't die was a complication he didn't need. He'd learned the hard way that sexual attraction could blind a man to the truth.

"Look at the tin ceiling," he said. "This place used to be a bank. We're standing where the customers would have come to speak to tellers."

Mazie put her hands on her hips. Slowly she turned around, taking in every angle, occasionally pausing to use her smartphone to snap a picture. "It's lovely," she said.

The comment was grudging. He knew that much. But at least she was honest.

"Thanks. I was lucky to get it. Had to scare off a guy who wanted to use it for an indoor miniature golf range."

"Surely you're joking."

"Not really. I'd like to think he'd never have been able to get the permits, but who knows?"

"You mentioned storage?"

"Ah, yes. There's a finished basement below us, small but nice. And more of the same above. The best part for you, though? There's a safe. We'll have to bring in an expert to get it working again. But you should be able to secure your high ticket items overnight, and thus eliminate any concerns about theft when you're not open."

When he showed her the ten-foot-square safe—stepping aside for her to enter—she lifted an eyebrow. "Kind of overkill, don't you think? My jewelry is small. I don't need nearly this much room."

He followed her in. "Not the way you do it now. But you've been removing every item and putting it all back each morning. If you use the shelves in this safe, you can carry entire trays in here at night and save yourself a ton of hassle."

Mazie pursed her lips. "True."

Her lips were red today, cherry red. It was impossible not to think about those lips wrapped around his—

"Tell me, J.B.," she said, interrupting his heated train of thought. "Is a bank safe this old really secure?"

He swallowed against a dry throat. "Well, it hasn't been used in some time but…"

Mazie pushed on the door. "It's crazy heavy. I suppose it would make a good hurricane shelter, too."

The door was weighted more efficiently than it seemed. Before J.B. could intervene, it slipped out of her grasp and slammed shut with a loud *thunk*.

The sudden pitch-black dark was disorienting.

Mazie's voice was small. "Oops. Guess I should have asked if you have the keys."

"Doesn't matter," he said. "They told me this thing isn't operational." He stepped forward cautiously. "Stand back. I'll grab the handle." That part was easy. Unfortunately, when he threw all his weight into it, nothing moved. "Damn."

He heard a rustle as Mazie shifted closer. "Isn't there a light?"

"Yeah." Reaching blindly, he slid his hand along the wall until he found the switch. The fluorescent bulb flickered, but came on.

Mazie stared at him, eyes huge. "I am *so* sorry. I didn't mean to close it."

"I know you didn't." His heart raced. Aside from the uncomfortable situation, he didn't want to get too close to Mazie. The two of them. In the dark. Very bad idea. "Don't worry," he said. "We'll be fine." He tried the handle a second time. Nothing budged. He pulled out his phone. "I'll call somebody."

He stared at the ominous words on the screen.

No service.

Of course there was no service. The vault was constructed of steel-reinforced concrete, designed to keep out intruders. And the building itself was of an era when walls were built several feet thick. The nearby coffee shop he frequented had terrible cell service because it also was housed in a historic structure.

"So you really *don't* have keys?" Mazie gnawed her lower lip, her arms wrapped around her waist.

"I have keys to the building. Not the safe."

"Someone will notice we're missing," she said. "Gina, anyway. She and I text twenty times a day. What about you? Did you tell anyone you were coming here?"

"I called your brother."

Mazie frowned. "Jonathan? Why?"

J.B. grimaced. "Because he knew I was having a hard time convincing you to sell. I told him you had agreed to at least consider this Queen Street property as an alternative."

"I see." She stared at him. "How often do you and my brother talk about me?"

"Almost never. Why would we?"

Mazie shrugged. "Maybe Jonathan will want to know whether or not you convinced me."

"If he calls, it will just go to voice mail. He'll assume I'm busy and leave a message."

"Well, that sucks." She exhaled sharply and kicked the wall. "You realize that if we die here, I'm going to haunt you for eternity."

"How can you haunt me if I'm dead, too?" He swiped a hand across his forehead, feeling the cold sweat. Her nonsense was a welcome distraction. He would focus on the woman in touching distance.

"Please don't ruin my fantasy," she said. "It's all I've got at the moment." She wrinkled her nose. "We don't even have a chair."

J.B. felt the walls move inward. He dragged in a lungful of air, but it was strangely devoid of oxygen. "Fine," he stuttered. "Feel free to haunt me."

Three

For the first time, Mazie noticed that J.B. seemed decidedly tense.

"Are you okay?" she asked, moving closer and putting a hand on his forehead.

She almost expected to find him burning up with fever, but he was cool as the proverbial cucumber. To her alarm, he didn't move away from her touch or offer even a token protest, and he didn't make some smart-ass remark.

"I'm fine," he said.

"You're definitely not fine."

She got in front of him and put both hands on his face. "Tell me what's wrong. You're scaring me."

His entire body was rigid.

He swallowed, the muscles in his throat rippling visibly. "I'm a tad claustrophobic. I might need you to hold me."

Fat chance. Her heart stumbled at his teasing. And then she remembered. When J.B. was eight years old, he'd been playing in a junkyard with some friends and had accidentally gotten closed up in an old refrigerator during a game of hide-and-seek. He had nearly died.

The incident traumatized him, understandably so. His parents had hired a therapist who came weekly to their house for over a year, but some deep wounds were hard to shake.

She stroked his hair, telling herself she was being kind and not reveling in the chance to touch him. "We're going to be okay. And I'm here, J.B. Take off your jacket. Let's sit down."

At first she wasn't sure he even processed what she was saying. But after a moment, he nodded, removed his sport coat, and slid down the wall until he sat on his butt with his legs outstretched. He sighed deeply. "I'm not going to flake out on you," he muttered.

"I never thought you would." She joined him, but it was far less graceful. Her skirt was unforgiving. She shimmied it up her thighs and managed to sit down without exposing too much.

For an eternity, it seemed, they said nothing. J.B.'s hands rested on his thighs, fists clenched. He was breathing too fast.

Mazie was no shrink. But even she knew he needed to get his mind on something else besides their predicament. "How are your parents?" she asked.

J.B. snorted and shot her a sideways glance. "Really, Mazie? I'm having an embarrassingly public meltdown, and that's the best you can do?"

"You're not having a meltdown," she said. "You're fine."

Maybe if she said it convincingly enough, he would believe her. They were sitting shoulder-to-shoulder, hip-to-hip with less than twelve inches separating them. It was the closest she had been to J.B. in forever. Close enough for her to catch an intoxicating whiff of his aftershave mixed with the entirely ordinary and yet exhilarating man smell of him.

He was big and strong and darkly masculine. Her stomach quivered. *This* was exactly why she normally kept her distance.

J.B. was dangerous.

When she glanced toward the ceiling, she saw tiny air vents up above. They were in no danger of suffocating. Even so, J.B.'s response was understandable. Her skin crawled, too, at the thought of being stuck here for hours.

J.B. was expending every ounce of concentration on not surrendering to the phobia. So any chitchat or small talk would have to be initiated by *her*. The trouble was, she knew J.B. too well, and not well enough.

Charleston wasn't that big a place. Anytime there was a charity gala or a gallery showing or a theater opening, Charleston's elite gathered. Over the years, Mazie had seen J.B. in formal wear on dozens of occasions, usually with a gorgeous woman on his arm. Not ever the same woman, but still…

Because he and Jonathan were best buds, she had also seen J.B. half-naked on the deck of a sailboat and at the basketball court and by the beach. If she really applied herself to the task, she could probably come up with a million and one times she had been in the same vicinity as J.B. and yet never exchanged two words with him.

That was her choice. And probably his. He had been inexplicably cruel to her at a vulnerable point in her life, and she had hated him ever since.

Now here they were. Stuck. Indefinitely.

The tile floor underneath her butt was cold and hard. She drew her knees up to her chest and circled them with her arms. J.B. was right beside her. It wasn't like he was going to look up her skirt.

She sighed. "You doin' okay, stud?" His shallow breathing was audible.

"Peachy."

The growled word, laden with surly testosterone, made her grin. "Why have you never married again?"

The words flew from her lips like starlings disturbed by a chimney sweep. They swirled outward and upward and hung in the air. *Oh, crap.*

Her muscles were paralyzed. Out of the corner of her eye she saw J.B.'s head come up. He went perfectly still. Not looking at her. Gazing straight ahead. The seconds ticked by. A minute passed. Maybe two.

"My parents are well," he said.

It took half a second for the subtext to process, and then she burst into laughter. "Very funny. Message received. The oh-so-mysterious J.B. Vaughan doesn't talk about his private life."

"Maybe I don't have a private life," he said. "Maybe I'm a workaholic who spends every waking hour trying to coax beautiful jewelry merchants into selling their property to me."

With one carefully placed adjective, the dynamic in the room changed. J.B. added flirtation to the mix. Did he do it on purpose? Or was he so accustomed to schmoozing women that the word *beautiful* slipped out?

She pretended not to hear. "If you're a workaholic at this age, you'll be dead before you're fifty. Why do you work so hard, J.B.? Didn't you ever want to stop and smell the roses?"

"I tried it once. Roses have thorns." He sucked in a breath of air. "Are you going to give me your property or not?"

"Did you lock me in here on purpose to make me say yes?"

"God, no. Even I'm not that desperate. Try *your* phone," he said. "You use a different carrier. Maybe it makes a difference."

She glanced at her cell. "Nope. Nada."

J.B. groaned. "How long have we been in here?"

Mazie peered at her watch. "Twenty-two minutes."

"Maybe your watch stopped."

She reached out and squeezed his hand. "Think about something else. Do you have all your Christmas shopping done? What do your sisters want?" J.B.'s two siblings were both younger and female. That's probably why he spent so much time hanging around the Tarleton house when he was growing up.

"They're great," he said. "Do we have to do this?"

"You're the one who didn't want to talk about anything serious."

"Are those my only two choices?"

She hesitated half a beat. "We *could* talk about why you were such an ass to me when we were teenagers."

J.B. cursed beneath his breath and leaped to his feet. "Maybe we shouldn't talk at all."

For the next five minutes, he paced the small space like a tiger in a cage. Mazie stayed where she was.

His body language shouted louder than words that he was unraveling.

At last, he paused in front of the impregnable door and slammed it with his fist. He bowed his head, his shoulders taut.

"I can't breathe," he whispered.

The agony in those three words twisted her heart. J.B. was a proud, arrogant man. Having her witness his weakness would make his frustration and anger and helplessness worse.

Without overthinking it, she scooted to her feet and went to him. "Listen to me." Fluorescent lighting was the most unflattering lighting in the world. It made both of them look like hell. His skin was sallow, cheekbones sharply etched. She took his face in her hands again. "Look at me. I want you to kiss me, J.B. Like you mean it. If you can't breathe, I might as well join you. Do it, big guy. Make me breathless. I dare you."

He was shaking, fine tremors that racked his body. But gradually, her words penetrated. "You want me to kiss you?"

"I do," she said. "More than anything." She touched her lips. "Right here. I haven't been kissed in ages. Show me how J.B. Vaughan woos a woman."

He blinked and frowned, as if sensing danger. "You're not serious."

She went up on her tiptoes and brushed her mouth over his. "Oh, yes I am. I'm so damn serious it ought to be against the law." She slid her fingers into his silky hair, cupping his skull, massaging his neck. "Kiss me, J.B."

If this worked, she was going to write a book about curing claustrophobia.

His hands landed on her shoulders, but she wasn't entirely sure he knew what he was doing. There was still a glassy-eyed element to his gaze.

"Mazie?" The way he said her name made the hair on her nape stand up. She knew exactly the moment his arousal broke through the grip of the visceral fear.

This time, the shudder that racked him was entirely hedonistic.

She didn't have to ask again for a kiss.

J.B. took control as if he had been kissing her always. His mouth settled over hers with a drugging sensuality that took the starch out of her knees and left her panting and helpless in his embrace.

Her arms linked around his neck. "This is nice."

"Screw nice…"

His rough laugh curled her toes. No wonder she had kept her distance all these years. At some level she had always known this could happen. She wanted to kick off her shoes and drag him to the floor, but everything was dusty and cold and hard. Not a soft surface in sight.

Once upon a time she had fantasized often about kissing J.B. Vaughan. The reality far outstripped her imaginings.

He was confident and coaxing and sexy and sweet, and she wanted to give him everything he asked for without words.

Thank God there wasn't a bed in sight. Otherwise, she might have done something really stupid.

His tongue stroked hers lazily. "I know what you're doing, and I don't even care. I should have kissed you years ago."

"You did," she reminded him.

"That didn't count. We were kids."

"Felt pretty grown-up to me." In fact, the adult J.B. was reacting much as the teenage J.B. had. His erection pressed against her belly, making her feel hot and dizzy and very confused.

This wasn't real. All she was doing was taking his mind off their incarceration.

He tugged her shirt loose and slid his hand up her back, unfastening her bra with one practiced flick of his fingers. Stroking her spine, he destroyed her bit by bit. "I always knew it would be like this," he groaned.

"Like what?" The two words were a whisper, barely audible over the loud pounding of her heart.

"Wild. Spectacular. Incredibly good." He put just enough space between them to let him cup her breasts in his hands. "Ah, Mazie."

His hands were warm. When he thumbed her nipples, the rough caress sent fire streaking throughout her body.

"Wait," she said. "My turn." She tugged at his soft shirt and sighed when she uncovered his muscled rib cage and taut abdomen. He was smooth and hard and had just enough silky hair to be interesting. She stopped short of his belt buckle.

J.B. nibbled the side of her neck. "Have you ever had sex standing up?"

"Um, no." Her brain was screaming at her to slow things down, but other parts of her body were having so much fun that sensible Mazie didn't stand a chance. "Have you?"

"No. I think it's one of those movie things that might not be so great in real life." He paused, his chest heaving. "But I'm willing to give it a try."

This was insane. They had gone from Mazie trying

to distract J.B. from his claustrophobia to jumping each other's bones at warp speed. Though she knew it was suicidal, she couldn't seem to stop herself.

"Kiss me again," she begged. Anything to keep his mind off doing something they both would surely regret.

He granted her wish and then some. First it was her breasts. He bent and tasted each one with murmurs of approval that did great things for her self-esteem. Then he moved up to her neck and her earlobes, and finally, her lips.

Oh, wow, the man knew how to kiss. She didn't even care how many women he had practiced on. The result was mesmerizing.

There were really only so many ways a man and a woman could put their lips together. Yet somehow, J.B. managed to make each ragged breath and groaning caress new and desperate.

He tasted her, and shuddered when she slipped her tongue between his lips and returned the favor. Need— hot and heavy—poured through her limbs and pulsed in her sex. It had been an eternity since she had experienced this level of arousal. Suddenly, she knew she would die if she couldn't have him right here, right now.

Trembling and weak, she clung to his broad shoulders. "I'm not on the Pill," she said. "I don't have any protection."

He bit her bottom lip, tugging it, turning her legs to spaghetti.

"Condom," he moaned. "Wallet."

"Yes." One part of her stood as an onlooker, marveling at her reckless behavior.

Really, Mazie? J.B. Vaughan? After he shot you down all those years ago and ignored you ever since?

Do you really want to do this?

She did. She really did. Maybe she always had.

J.B. removed her top and bra and draped them carefully over the door handle of the safe. Then he turned and stared at her.

She crossed her arms over her chest, unable to pretend sophistication. There had been two men in her life. Not a big number.

He ran his hand from her bare shoulder down her arm, manacling her wrist and reeling her in. "You're exquisite, Mazie."

The recollection of a teenage J.B. had always messed with her head. The popular boy with the raw sexuality and the wicked grin had rejected her and made her feel less than feminine, less than desirable.

It was difficult to reconcile that memory with the present.

"I'm glad you think so."

His slight frown told her he recognized her equivocation. He kissed her temple.

"I love your hair." He ran his hands through it. "It bounces with life and passion. Like you, Mazie."

The sudden segue from frantic hunger to tenderness unsettled her. It was one thing to get caught up in the moment. She didn't trust J.B.'s quiet gentleness. A man could use sex to get what he wanted. Maybe in the midst of their madness, J.B. had recognized her vulnerability where he was concerned. Maybe he hoped to use it to his advantage.

"Kiss me again," she begged. Boldly, she cupped the length of his sex through his pants. He was hard and ready, so ready that the evidence made her want to swoon like some fainthearted Victorian maiden.

Mazie had been abstinent by choice for the past two years. No man had tempted her, not even a little. Now here was J.B. All wrong for her in every way. But at the moment, oh so right.

When she touched him intimately, he shuddered. This time, she knew the tremors that racked his big frame had nothing to do with a fear of enclosed spaces. J.B. wanted her. Badly. The realization was exhilarating.

They were still mostly clothed, though her bare breasts nestled delightfully against his warm, hard chest. It should have felt weird and odd to be standing here like this. Instead, it was the most wonderfully terrifying thing in the world. In his embrace, she felt torn in a dozen dizzying directions.

She hated this man. Didn't she? Or was this a delightful dream?

The illusion was worth any price. She had waited a decade and more for J.B. to admit that he wanted her. Surely the fates would grant her one outrageous walk on the wild side.

She could call it off. The end would be ugly and awkward and far more scarring than what had happened when she was sixteen. But J.B. would never force himself on a woman, even if Mazie had been the one to initiate the encounter.

"I want you, darlin' Mazie." When he whispered her name and touched her thigh beneath her skirt, she knew the moment was at hand.

It was no contest. "I want you, too, J.B."

What happened next was sheer madness. He

scooped her up and backed her against the wall. Her hands tangled in his hair. They were both panting as if they had run a marathon.

He cupped her bottom, grinding his lower half against hers until she wanted to scream with frustration.

He slid his hands beneath her skirt and found bare skin. "Put your legs around my waist."

"The condom," she said. "Don't forget the condom."

"In a minute." He kissed her wildly, his teeth bruising her lips. She pulled his hair, fighting to get closer. Her bikini panties were damp. Her entire body wept with the need to have him inside her.

She crossed her ankles behind his back, ripping at his shirt. "Take this off," she pleaded.

He managed it without breaking the kiss. Now she could run her hands over acres of warm male skin. His body was toned and tanned and sleekly muscled. For a man who supposedly spent a lot of time with spreadsheets and architectural plans, he had the build of an athlete.

"Hang on tight," he demanded. With a muffled groan, he ripped her underpants and held the scraps aloft. "Mission accomplished."

"Those were new," she protested.

J.B.'s grin was feral. "I'll buy you more."

Now he could go where no man had gone in a very long time. He caressed her intimately, inserting one finger...feeling the embarrassingly welcome state of her sex.

"Oh, wow..." She dropped her head to his shoulder and closed her eyes.

J.B. chuckled. "If you like that, I've got lots more."

Without warning, a thunderous pounding on the huge door reverberated in the enclosed space. A muffled shout sounded. "Anybody in there?"

"Holy damn. Lord have mercy."

J.B.'s incredulous response would have been hysterically funny if Mazie hadn't been poised on the brink of a really spectacular orgasm. She groaned and buried her face in his neck.

The voice came again. "Stand back. I'm going to open the door."

"Oh, my God." She jerked out of J.B.'s arms and grabbed for her bra and shirt.

J.B. stared at her, his gaze hot enough to melt all of her inhibitions. "Saved by the bell..."

She should be glad—right? Glad that she hadn't done something stupid and self-destructive?

What was he thinking? His expression was grim.

Her heart sank, incredulous at the way she had let herself fall into old patterns. Suddenly, the situation seemed a thousand times worse.

Four

J.B. cursed beneath his breath, stunned at his run of bad luck. Then again, maybe he should admit the truth. No matter his physical frustration, he had escaped certain catastrophe. He'd spent years avoiding Mazie Tarleton, and yet he'd come perilously close to doing the very thing he knew he couldn't do.

His beautiful enemy was barely decent when a loud scraping ensued, and the heavy door began to swing inward. At the last second, J.B. shoved her torn underwear into his pocket and slipped his shirt on again.

The lights from outside the vault were so bright they both blinked. Their rescuer crossed his arms over his chest. Jonathan Tarleton. Mazie's brother. With a smug smile on his face. "Well, look at you two."

J.B. took a step forward, shielding Mazie in case she had anything else she needed to tuck away. "What are you doing here?"

Jonathan moved back, allowing them to exit. "I though maybe I could convince Mazie to give you a fair hearing. When I arrived, I saw both of your cars, but neither of you. So I put my CSI skills to work and found footprints leading to the vault. Fortunately for you, this hardwood floor is dusty as hell."

For J.B., the rush of cool air was blissful. He inhaled deeply, feeling the last tentacles of his brief ordeal slip away.

Truth be told, Mazie had rescued him quite effectively. Her methods were almost beguiling enough to make him drag her back into the vault and shut the door again.

Almost, but not quite.

"Thanks for rescuing us," he said. "If you hadn't come by, we might have spent an uncomfortable few hours locked up in there."

"The mechanism was jammed on the outside. I had to hit it with my shoe to knock it loose."

Mazie hadn't said a word up until now, though she had hugged her brother briefly. She edged toward the front of the building. "It was my fault. I didn't mean to close the door." She grimaced. "Not to be rude, but I'm in dire need of the ladies' room. I'll see you later, Jonathan." She gave J.B. an oddly guarded look for someone who had only recently been wrapped around him like a feather boa. "Thanks for the tour."

And then she was gone.

He stared out the window, wondering if the sick feeling in the pit of his stomach was sexual disappointment or something far more alarming.

Had he actually *connected* with his prickly nemesis? Surely not. He couldn't. He wouldn't. The only reason he was spending time with her at all was to seal a deal. He dared not let himself get sidetracked by an almost irresistible attraction.

That kind of thing made a man stupid. He should know.

Jonathan cuffed his shoulder. "Well," he said. "Did you convince her? What did she say?"

J.B. ran his hands through his hair. "She didn't say anything. We'd barely started looking the place over when we got stuck. I have no idea if she liked it or not."

"Of course she liked it," Jonathan said. "Mazie is a sucker for historic buildings. This one has tons of original features, but unlike the dump she's in now, your building is rock-solid."

"Yeah." J.B. nodded absently, reliving every incredible moment of his incarceration. Now that it was over, the whole thing seemed like a dream. Did Mazie Tarleton really let him touch her and nearly make love to her?

"Hey, J.B." Jonathan eyed him strangely.

"What?"

"You have lipstick on your chin."

J.B. froze inwardly. This was a minefield. Mazie wasn't a child anymore, but Jonathan was very protective. That was part of the reason J.B. had kept a healthy distance from her over the years. "Do I?" he said.

Jonathan's expression segued into a frown. "What the hell went on in that vault?"

"None of your damn business. Your sister is an adult. Besides, nothing happened. I got claustrophobic, and Mazie tried to distract me with a little kiss."

"Claustrophobic?" Jonathan's distrust vanished. "Oh, man, J.B., I'm sorry. You must have freaked. That was nice of her, especially considering she doesn't like you all that much."

She seemed to like me just fine a few minutes ago when she had her tongue down my throat.

J.B. swallowed the sarcastic words and managed a noncommittal nod. "Not my finest hour. It's humiliating as hell to have something that happened almost twenty-five years ago still yank my chain. For a minute in there, I thought I was going to lose it."

"You should be glad it was Mazie with you and not someone else. At least she won't ever tease you about it. That girl has a tender heart."

"She's a lot like Hartley in that way. The two of them were always bringing home strays. Have you heard from him at all? I still can't believe he simply vanished."

"No. But it's only a matter of time. Hartley was born and bred here. The Lowcountry is in his blood."

"You don't sound happy about that."

"He abandoned the family business…left me to deal with Dad. I don't have a lot of sympathy for my brother right now."

"He's your twin. Twins are close."

"We were at one time. Not anymore."

"You say that, Jonathan, but I know you. And I know Hartley. The two of you were practically inseparable when we were growing up. You can't pretend that tie isn't there. It always will be."

"Not if I don't want it…not if I don't want *him*."

J.B. let the subject drop, but only because he saw beneath Jonathan's angry response to the deep hurt that still festered.

He rotated his shoulders and took one last look

around the room. "I think this will work for Mazie. I didn't get a firm *yes* from her, but I'll follow up."

"And I'll continue to put in a good word for you."

They exited the building. J.B. locked up. "You on for basketball next weekend?"

"Yeah. Seven o'clock?"

J.B. nodded. "I'll see you then."

When Jonathan climbed in his car and drove away, J.B. should have followed suit, but he felt oddly out of sorts. Perhaps because he wanted to get this project settled. He needed Mazie's property.

Who was he kidding? Every bit of his current angst was because of a frustrating, completely off-limits woman who had bedeviled him for years. He wanted her. End of story.

He took out his phone and pulled up her contact info. A short text in this situation would be perfectly acceptable.

Hope you liked the property. Let me know what you think.

But he couldn't do it. Mazie had muddied the waters. Or maybe they both had. He was accustomed to closing deals. In business. For pleasure. Never both at the same time.

This was exactly why he was screwed. He had resisted temptation all this time, and then in one short afternoon he'd undone all his good intentions.

Thinking about Mazie was a mistake. Half an hour ago, he had been primed to make love to her. His body had been denied satisfaction, and now he was itchy, restless.

One thing he knew for sure.

Kissing Mazie Tarleton was an experience he

planned to repeat. Some way. Somehow. Maybe *she* didn't know it, but J.B.'s intentions were crystal clear.

Now that he had touched her, tasted her, there was no going back…

Mazie wanted to go straight home and take a long cold shower, but it was too early in the day to be done with work, and besides, Gina was expecting her to return.

There was no choice but to brazen it out.

Which was not easy when a girl was commando under her skirt.

Fortunately, the shop was swamped with customers. Mazie barely did more than wave at Gina and say hello to her other employees before she was pulled into the fray. Thank goodness for tour ships that dispatched groups of passengers ashore, eager to tick off items on their Christmas lists.

At last, the furor subsided. Mazie sent two of her employees on lunch break. She glanced at her watch. It was almost one.

Mazie had advertised heavily during the last year in several of the cruise lines' brochures. Her print ads were paying off, despite the digital age. Today, she'd had several customers come in clutching their maps of the historic district. All That Glitters was clearly marked, along with the small rectangle showcasing a beautiful necklace and the store's phone number with other contact info.

She glanced in one of the larger cases. "We're going to need more sweetgrass basket charms in gold."

Gina nodded. "Yep. One lady bought six of them

for her granddaughters. I'll call Eve this afternoon and place an order."

They were eating pizza standing up, a common occurrence. Gina swallowed a bite and grinned. "Don't keep me in suspense. How did it go with Mr. Gorgeous? Did you like the building?"

"Honestly, I did. The place J.B. wants us to have was originally a nineteenth-century bank. He was showing me the vault when we had a little accident and got locked inside."

Gina's eyes rounded. "You got locked in a bank vault with J.B. Vaughan? God, that's so romantic."

"Um, no. Not romantic at all." You couldn't call what happened with J.B. romance. Sexual frenzy, maybe.

"So it was too scary to be romantic?"

The other woman's crestfallen expression might have been funny if Mazie hadn't been walking on eggshells. She wasn't going to betray J.B.'s secret weakness. Instead, she skirted the truth. "Not so much scary as tense. We were awfully glad to get out of there when Jonathan showed up."

"So are you going to take it? The building, I mean? Will it work for our purposes?"

"It's perfect. Doesn't mean I'm ready to give J.B. what he wants. Surely there's another way."

"Has anyone ever told you that you're contrary?"

"You," Mazie said, finishing her meal. "Every other day." She wiped her hands on a napkin. "My...*conversation* with J.B. got derailed when my brother showed up. I'm sure I'll hear from him soon. J.B., that is."

"And what will you say when he asks you again?"

Mazie flashed to a mental image of the real estate

developer's chest. His tousled hair. His eyes, heavy-lidded with desire. Her throat tightened. Her thighs pressed together. "I don't really know."

Unfortunately, the afternoon crowd picked up, and Mazie never found a moment to scoot home and restock her wardrobe. By the time the shop closed at five, she was more than ready to call it quits.

The Tarleton family had lived for decades on the tip of a small barrier island just north of the city. They owned fifteen acres, more than enough to create a compound that included the main house and several smaller buildings scattered around.

An imposing, gated iron fence protected the enclave on land. Water access was impossible due to a high brick wall Mazie's grandfather had erected at the top of the sand. The beach itself was public property, but he had made sure no one could wander onto Tarleton property, either out of curiosity or with dangerous motives. Hurricanes and erosion made the wall outrageously expensive to maintain, but the current Tarleton patriarch was by nature paranoid and suspicious, so security was a constant concern.

At times, Mazie felt unbearably strangled by her familial obligations. Perhaps that was why being around J.B. felt both dangerous and exhilarating all at the same instant.

She punched her security code into the keypad and waited for the heavy gate to slide open. She and Jonathan both wanted to move out, but they were trapped by the weight of love and responsibility for their father. She suspected her brother kept an apartment in the city so he could have a private life, but she didn't pry. Someday she might find a place of her own, as well.

She had let the long-ago debacle with J.B. cast too long a shadow over her romantic life. Heartbreak had made her overly cautious.

It was time to find some closure with J.B., one way or another. Time to move on.

The house where she had grown up was a colossal structure of sandstone and timber, on stilts, of course. Supposedly, it had been built to withstand a Category Four hurricane. Though the family home had suffered damage over the years, the original structure was still mostly intact.

An imposing front staircase swept upward to double mahogany doors inlaid with stained glass. The images of starfish and dolphins and sea turtles had fascinated her as a child. When she grew tall enough, she liked to stand on the porch and trace them with her fingertips.

The sea creatures were free in a way that Mazie couldn't imagine. All her life she had been hemmed in by her mother's illness and later, her father's paranoia. Jonathan and Hartley—when they had been in a mood to tolerate her—had been her companions, her best friends.

And J.B., too.

The Vaughan family was one of only a handful in Charleston as wealthy as the Tarletons, so Gerald Tarleton had condoned, even promoted his children's friendship with J.B. But Mazie was younger, and Hartley was a loner, so it was always Jonathan and J.B. who were the closest.

Mazie had adored J.B. as a child, then had a crush on him as a teenager, and finally, hated him for years.

No matter how she examined her past, it was impossible to excise J.B. from the memories.

Mazie found her father in the large family room with the double plate-glass windows. The ocean was benign today, shimmering shades of blue and turquoise stretching all the way to the horizon.

"Hi, Daddy." She kissed the top of his curly, white-haired head. Her father was reading the *Wall Street Journal*, or pretending to. More often than not, she discovered him napping. Gerald Tarleton had been an imposing figure at one time. Tall and barrel-chested, he could bluster and intimidate with the best of them.

As he aged, he had lost much of his fire.

He reached up and patted her hand. "There you are, pumpkin. Will you tell cook I want dinner at six thirty instead of seven?"

"Of course. Did you have a good day?"

"Stupid doctor says I can't smoke cigars anymore. Where's the fun in that?"

The family physician made twice yearly visits to the Tarleton compound. Mazie wasn't sorry to have missed this one. "He's trying to keep you alive."

"Or take away my reasons for living," he groused comically.

Her father had married later in life, a man in his midforties taking a much younger bride. The story wasn't so unusual. But in Gerald's case, it had ended tragically. His bride and her parents had hidden from him the extent of her mental struggles, leaving Gerald to eventually raise his young family on his own.

Mazie and her brothers had each paid an invisible price that followed them into adulthood.

She ignored his mood. "I'll speak to cook, and then

I'm going to change clothes. I'll be back down in half an hour or so."

"And Jonathan?"

"He's home tonight, I think."

After a quick word with the woman who ran the kitchen like a drill sergeant, but with sublime culinary skills, Mazie ran upstairs and at last made it to the privacy of her bedroom. She stripped off her clothes, trying not to think about J.B.'s hands on her body.

His touch had opened her eyes to several disturbing truths, not the least of which was that she had carried a tendresse for him, an affection, that had never been stamped out.

She had spent a semester in France her senior year, only a few months after he had rejected her. The entire time she was abroad, she had imagined herself wandering the streets of Paris with J.B.

What a foolish, schoolgirl dream.

Yet now, when she stared in the mirror and saw her naked body, it was impossible to separate her former daydreams from the inescapable reality. She had allowed J.B. Vaughan to caress her breasts, to touch her intimately.

Had Jonathan not intruded to *rescue* them, would she have regrets?

Confusion curled her stomach. She wasn't the kind of person who jumped into bed with a man. Especially not J.B.

Something had happened in the vault.

Yet however she replayed the sequence of events, J.B. didn't come out the villain. *Mazie* had been the one to accidentally close the door and lock them in. *Mazie* had been the one to kiss J.B. *Mazie* had been the one who decided that a nod to her past infatuation would serve to distract J.B. from his claustrophobia.

Was it any wonder he had taken her invitation and run with it?

She stayed in the shower a long time, scrubbing and scrubbing again, trying to erase every vestige of his touch from her skin. She still wanted to hate him. He was still off-limits. And damn it, she *still* wanted to see him squirm.

Today had weakened her position in their face-off.

J.B. was a highly sexual man. When a woman gave him every indication she *wanted* sex, it was no wonder he had obliged.

Mazie had to live with the knowledge that she had done something extremely foolhardy. Self-destructive even.

Circumstances had saved her from the ultimate humiliation.

She didn't have to face J.B. as an ex-lover. Thank God for that.

But the unseen damage was worse, perhaps.

Now she knew what it felt like to be in his arms, to hear him whisper her name in a ragged groan that sent shivers of raw pleasure down her spine. Tonight when she climbed into bed, she would remember his hands on her breasts, her bare body, her sex.

How could she think about anything else?

Five

Even now, her hands trembled as she dried herself with a huge fluffy towel that smelled of sunshine and ocean breezes. The housekeeper liked pinning the laundry on an old-fashioned clothesline when weather permitted.

Mazie put on soft, faded jeans and a periwinkle cashmere sweater with a scoop neck. A short strand of pearls that had been her mother's dressed up the outfit enough to meet her father's old-school dinner requirements.

Sooner or later, J.B. would call about the property swap. She would have to speak to him as if nothing out of the ordinary had happened. And she would have to give him an answer.

His offer was generous. There was no denying the truth.

But she didn't want to give him what he wanted.

Though it was childish and petty on her part, something inside her wanted to hurt him as much as he had hurt her. For J.B., that meant she needed to hurt his business. She was certain he didn't have a heart or real emotions. All he cared about was stacking up more money and more accolades for his financial acumen.

If he really cared about *her*, he'd had plenty of years to make up for the past. But he hadn't.

At last, she could delay no longer. The sun had set in a blaze of glory, and darkness had fallen over the island. She heard a car in the driveway and recognized her brother's voice as it floated up from the foyer.

This mess with J.B. would have to wait.

She had time. Time to come up with a plan. When she saw him again, she wanted to be in control.

Passionless.

Absolutely calm.

There was a very good chance he had used their interlude in the vault to sway her to his side. Though he had not instigated the encounter, he was intuitive and fiercely intelligent. If he had sensed her weakness where he was concerned, he wouldn't have hesitated to use it against her. Nor would he in the future.

She had to be on her guard. She couldn't let her vulnerabilities where J.B. was concerned fool her into thinking he might really care about her.

Troubled and unsettled, she made her way downstairs. Jonathan might quiz her about the incident earlier in the day when she and J.B. had been trapped, but her father would be oblivious. If the subject came up, she would steer the conversation in a safer direction.

She walked into the dining room, ruefully aware that as usual, the full complement of china and silver and crystal adorned the table. A low arrangement of red roses and holly nestled in a Waterford bowl. Despite the fact that there were only three of them, the Tarletons would dine in style.

Grimacing inwardly, she stopped short when she saw the fourth place setting.

"Who's coming to dinner?" she asked Jonathan, a dreadful premonition already shaking her foundations.

Behind her, a familiar velvet-smooth voice replied.

"It's me," J.B. said. "I hope you don't mind another mouth to feed."

J.B. was accustomed to women's flirtatious maneuvers and their attempts to secure his attention. Rarely had he seen a woman with an expression on her face like Mazie's. She recovered quickly, but for a split second, she was startled, her unguarded look revealing a mixture of dismay and sensual awareness.

He'd be lying if he said the dismay didn't puncture his ego. Nevertheless, he kept his smile.

Mazie circled the room, keeping the dinner table between them. "Of course not. This is my father's house. There's always room for one more."

Gerald and Jonathan sat at the head and foot of the table, leaving J.B. and Mazie to face each other from opposite sides. Just for the hell of it, he moved quickly to hold out Mazie's chair as she took her seat. At the last moment, he unobtrusively brushed the side of her neck with a fleeting touch.

He was almost positive she inhaled a sharp breath, but Gerald was talking in a loud voice, so J.B. couldn't be sure. When the four of them were in place, the housekeeper brought out the first course.

By any culinary standards, it was an amazing meal. The Tarletons' cook was more akin to a chef, and she specialized in Lowcountry dishes that included the best of Charleston's local seafood. Tonight's offering was shrimp and grits with a Caesar salad on the side. J.B. was hungry, so he ate well.

But simmering beneath the surface of the lively conversation was the knowledge that Mazie never once looked him straight in the eye. Nor did she address a single comment directly to him. Her behavior was frustrating.

Things were different between them now…whether Mazie liked it or not.

While J.B. nursed his growing indignation, Gerald Tarleton dominated the evening's debate. Despite his declining health, he continued to go into work every day. He and Jonathan commanded a vast shipping empire that had made the family even more wealthy than it had been in the early days when Gerald took over the reins from *his* father.

At one point, J.B. caught his host's attention. "Mr. Tarleton, my dad wanted me to extend an invitation. He'd love to take you out deep-sea fishing on his new boat."

Gerald shook his head, sipping his wine and for a moment looking oddly fragile. "Tell him thanks, boy. But I don't get out and about much anymore. These old bones give me fits. And call me Gerald. You're not a kid anymore."

"The boat is a honey, Gerald. Almost as comfortable as my own house. The crew would pamper you. Think about it, why don't you? Dad respects you a great deal.

I know it would tickle him to have a chance to pick your brain about business."

Gerald's pleased expression told J.B. that he had made inroads into the old man's instinctive refusal.

J.B. turned his attention to Mazie. "What about you, Mazie Jane? I seem to recall that you like to fish. We could make a party of it." He tried to get a rise out of her. Mazie had always hated her full name, because she thought it was too old-fashioned.

She choked on a bite of shrimp. Had to dab her mouth with a napkin before she could answer.

"Sounds fun," she said, clearly lying. "If I can find a free Saturday, I'll let you know."

Her Saturdays would be free when hell froze over. That much J.B. knew.

She was blowing him off, and none too subtly. Her evasion brought out his fighting instincts.

Jonathan's cell phone buzzed. He pulled it from his jacket pocket, gave his three companions an apologetic look and stood. "I have to deal with this. Sorry to interrupt the meal."

Cook spirited his plate away to keep the food warm.

Now it was only J.B., Mazie and an elderly man who was already nodding off, his chin on his chest.

J.B. crooked a finger. "I need to speak to you," he whispered. "In private." He motioned toward the door that led to the covered veranda.

Mazie glanced at her father and then at her plate. "I'm eating."

"This won't take long."

"I don't have anything to say to you."

"But I have things to say to *you*," he said firmly.

"Or I can wait until your brother returns, and he can hear it all."

"You're a bully," she said, but she rose to her feet. "Make this quick."

Quietly, they stepped outside onto the porch and closed the door behind them.

Mazie wrapped her arms around her waist. "What?" she asked. "What's so damned important?"

"I want to know why you're looking at me like gum you scraped off the bottom of your shoe."

"I'm not," she said, backing away from him half a step.

"Yes. You are. I'm not an idiot. This morning you and I were—"

She shoved a hand against his chest, halting his words in midsentence. "Stop it. Right there. This morning was a mistake." Then she backed up again, almost as if she were afraid to let herself get too close to him.

He lifted an eyebrow. "You didn't enjoy yourself?"

"That's beside the point. It shouldn't have happened. And it won't again."

He chewed on that for a moment. "What are you afraid of, honey?"

Her eyes flashed. "Typical male response. If a woman doesn't want you, she must be afraid. That's bull crap, J.B."

"No," he said, trying his best to tamp down his anger and frustration. "What's bull crap is you trying to pretend that something extraordinary didn't happen between us today…" He hesitated, unwilling to give her ammunition, but itching to get at the truth. "That kind of connection is rare, Mazie."

She stared at him, eyes wide, posture shouting her

unease. "I bet you use that line with a lot of women. You have a reputation, you know."

It was true. He couldn't deny it.

But her wariness went much farther back than that. Yes, he dated plenty of women. Mazie had made her judgments about him a long time ago, though.

"Have dinner with me tomorrow night," he said.

"Why? So you can badger me about my property?"

"Would you rather call it a date?"

He had boxed her into a momentary corner. Even as a child, Mazie never backed down from a dare. Now, he used that knowledge against her.

She lifted a shoulder and let it fall. "Fine," she said. "I'll meet you for a business dinner."

"I'll pick you up instead."

"Something casual."

"I'm taking you to Étoile de Mer."

"Absolutely not."

The French restaurant was intimate and extremely formal. In a century and a city that welcomed tourists in virtually any state of dress, Étoile de Mer maintained the old standards. Men in dinner jackets. Women in long dresses. Dancing beneath an antique Baccarat chandelier. The ambiance was unapologetically romantic and luxurious.

He smiled cajolingly. "It's December, Mazie. Jonathan talks about how much you enjoy the season. The hotel will be decorated to the nines. And Chef Marchon has a special holiday menu. The orchestra will play Christmas songs. Say yes. We'll have fun."

A tiny smile lifted the edges of her lips. "Do you always get your way?"

"Most of the time."

"Why are you doing this?" she asked.

He frowned. "I want to spend time with you. Is that so strange?" It *was* strange. And unprecedented. Both of them knew it. He was supposed to be closing a business deal, not chasing an attraction that could burn them both and end very badly.

He was her brother's best friend. It wasn't as if he could walk away and never see her again.

Her wariness was almost palpable. "I won't give you an answer about selling my property for a couple of weeks. I need time to think it over, to discuss the big picture with Gina. To decide how complicated it would be to move the store. If you're hoping to wine and dine me tomorrow night, so I'll be all mellow and sign on the dotted line, that's not going to happen."

"What if I said this wasn't about business at all?"

The words slipped out before he could snatch them back. To be honest, he hadn't known he was going to say something so revealing.

She put a hand to her throat, nervously playing with the strand of pearls. The necklace was nice, but if he had his way, the pearls would be an entire rope, and he would drape them around her neck while they were in bed.

Mazie made no move to break the silence, so he re-phrased the question. "What if I swear that tomorrow night will be entirely personal?"

"You're scaring me."

She said it with humor, but he took her words at face value. "Nothing scary, Mazie. Nothing at all. Just two friends enjoying dinner." He was lying through his teeth. This was about much more than dinner. He was courting danger.

"If this is about what happened in the vault, I have to tell you that I'm not usually so…"

Her wrinkled nose and wry embarrassment touched him. "You were incredible. I've had a hard-on the entire damn day."

"J.B.!"

Her mortified expression made him chuckle. "I get it, Mazie. You're telling me not to expect anything after dinner. That I get my dessert at the restaurant and not in my bed."

"You make me sound naive and ridiculous."

"You're neither of those things. But I'd be lying if I said you didn't shock me this morning. Hell, Mazie. I guess I've had sex a little more than you have, but you and me today…" He leaned against the porch railing and stared out at the ocean. The sound of the waves usually soothed him. Not tonight.

"What about us?"

There was a world of feminine emotion wrapped up in those three little words. Asking for reassurance.

"We connected," he muttered.

He didn't know how else to explain it. He couldn't even make sense of it himself. Was he headed down a familiar road? Letting sexual attraction drag him into a relationship that was doomed to failure?

"We should go back inside," she said quietly. "Jonathan will wonder where we are."

Something clicked. "Is Jonathan part of the problem? Are you worried about what your brother will think?"

"I don't want to cause discord between the two of you."

"Leave that to me." He sounded more confident than he felt.

Jonathan was likely to punch him, at the very least, if he found out J.B. was dallying with his baby sister. After all, Jonathan was partly to blame for the fact that Mazie had held a grudge against J.B. for so long.

"Daddy's awake," Mazie said. "I can see him waving his arms. Probably bossing the cook. Let's go in."

J.B. took her wrist, holding it lightly, needing to touch her, but not wanting to spook her. "I want to kiss you again."

"You do?"

"Yeah. Pretty badly. Just a kiss, Mazie. That's all."

Slowly, waiting for her to lean in and exhaling on a sigh of relief when she did, he drew her against his chest and wrapped his arms around her. She was tall for a woman. Their heights matched perfectly.

She was soft and warm. He buried his face in her neck, dragging oxygen into his lungs. Reminding himself he wasn't a horny teenager. He could control his emotions and his body.

When his mouth found hers, she murmured his name. Hearing her say it, all low and husky like that, made him nuts. He tangled a hand in her hair and deepened the kiss.

He hadn't imagined it. The fire. The wanting.

Whatever happened with Mazie in that bank vault this morning had nothing to do with his claustrophobia or a stress-induced jolt of adrenaline from being trapped.

It was all Mazie.

Now, she kissed him back. Unmistakably. When he would have pulled away, her hands clung to his shoulders, and she pressed against him. His erection was hard and heavy between them. Nothing he could do about that.

"Mazie," he croaked, trying to back away from the edge of insanity. "We need to go back inside. You said so. You're right."

"Don't listen to me," she said, unbuttoning a button on his shirt and stroking his collarbone.

The little tease was tormenting him on purpose.

He dragged her with him to a less exposed section of the veranda, around the corner of the house. This was not the time for Jonathan to burst through the doorway and find his sister in a compromising position.

"Enough," J.B. begged, wondering when exactly he had lost the upper hand. He batted her hand away and rebuttoned his shirt. "Say yes to tomorrow night. It's the only answer I'll accept."

She smiled up at him, her eyelids heavy, her lower lip plump and shiny where he had sucked on it. "Yes."

Something inside him settled. "And you'll wear a kick-ass dress so I can make all the other men jealous?"

"I want to dance with you," she said. "If we're going all out for this *date*, I'll expect dancing."

"Duly noted."

"And expensive champagne. Maybe even caviar."

"Yes, ma'am."

"I still don't know why we're doing this," she said, the humor fading from her voice. "It seems awfully dangerous. Southern mamas warn their daughters about men like you."

He rubbed his thumb over her cheek, cupping her face. "You should have had a mother, Mazie. I'm sorry about all you lost."

She pulled away from him as if the sudden switch to a serious topic was more than she could bear.

Though her back was to him now, he saw her shrug. "I was luckier than most kids. My father indulged me."

Sliding his arms around her from behind, he rested his chin on top of her head. "It's easy to do. I have the same tendency myself."

"Which doesn't explain why you're trying to steal my livelihood."

He snorted. "Cut the drama. Besides, we're shelving the business negotiations for now. Isn't that what you wanted?"

It was getting more and more difficult to tell himself that this new détente with Mazie was all about business.

She turned around and looked up at him. "We don't always get what we want, J.B."

Six

Mazie wanted another kiss. But she knew her limits. Already she was playing with fire. Common sense was no match for the beat of her heart and the yearning in her blood.

Could she pursue this attraction and not get hurt? Could she indulge in her passion for J.B. and yet still make him pay for all the pain he had caused her in the past?

She fled the porch, not waiting to see if J.B. followed. Fortunately, her father was enjoying his favorite dessert—warm peach cobbler with ice cream. And Jonathan still hadn't returned.

Her father looked up when she walked into the room. "I wondered where everybody had gone."

"You were dozing," she said, seating herself at the table and picking up the napkin. "J.B. and I were talking business."

Her father raised an eyebrow. "Is he trying to sell you something?"

"No, sir," Mazie said. "He wants to buy the building I'm in."

"Make him work for it."

J.B. sat down as well, smoothing his hair and giving Mazie a steely-eyed glance. "No worries there, sir. Your daughter drives a hard bargain."

Fortunately for Mazie, Jonathan returned at that moment, and she was able to consume her dessert in peace while the men grumbled about sports and politics and whether or not South Carolina was going to have a colder-than-normal winter.

It was the occasional heated glances from J.B. that kept her on edge. Even in the midst of male conversation, he made it clear that his thoughts were on her.

Soon after, J.B. said his goodbyes.

Mazie considered walking him out, but Jonathan beat her to it, so she stayed where she was, telling herself she wasn't disappointed. She had kissed J.B. Vaughan entirely too many times for one day.

When Jonathan came back inside, he shut the front door and began punching in numbers to set the alarm. Mazie stopped him. "Are you in the mood to walk the beach?" she asked in a low voice. "I need to talk to you about a couple of things, and I don't want to do it in the house where Daddy can hear."

Jonathan looked tired and stressed, but he nodded. "Sure. You do know it's December?"

It was a running joke between them. A sort of dare as to which of the two would cry uncle when the temperatures dropped. "I'll bundle up," she said.

As she found her earmuffs and a heavy scarf and

slipped on an old thigh-length coat, she couldn't help but wonder if J.B. would have welcomed an invitation to stay for a while. Had Jonathan not been home tonight, she might have been tempted.

On the way down the hall, she stopped by her father's bedroom.

"Jonathan and I are going for a walk on the beach," she said. "We won't be gone too long."

Her father lifted his head from his task and frowned. "It's not safe. I like having you both inside the house, so I know where you are."

She hugged him. "We need the exercise. Jonathan seems awfully stressed. Is everything okay at work?"

"The usual kerfuffles. He's fine."

"Have you heard anything at all from Hartley?"

Her father paled, his gaze haunted. "No. Go for your walk. And make sure you lock up when you get back."

"Yes, Daddy."

Jonathan was waiting for her. He tugged a toboggan over his head. "All set?"

She nodded. "Let's go."

In the brick wall on the back side of the house, a heavy wooden gate with electric voltage across the top provided an exit point. Jonathan disarmed the system and held the door for her to pass. In the soft powdery sand at this level, her feet slipped and slid. They crossed the beach to where the tide was going out, then turned left and started to walk.

Jonathan altered his stride to hers immediately. They found their rhythm and strode briskly. Occasionally, another intrepid beach walker passed by going in the opposite direction, but for the most part they had the beach to themselves.

Sometimes when they walked so late, they carried flashlights. This week, the nearly full moon provided plenty of illumination.

Mazie stared out at the almost invisible horizon. Tonight, the line between sea and sky was barely perceptible. As children, she and Hartley and Jonathan—and often J.B.—had loved watching the huge ships coming in and out of Charleston's historic harbor. They had learned how to spot Tarleton vessels, and how to read the bits of foreign language markings on others.

Often, especially on rainy days when there were no good outdoor activities to entertain a quartet of rambunctious children, they spun stories for each other about mysterious cargoes and whether or not it would be possible to stow away and make a sea voyage on the company's dime.

If they had been particularly well behaved, their father would bring out his expensive, high-powered binoculars and teach them how to focus the lenses. Mazie had stared at the ocean for as long as she could remember.

It was vast and inscrutable. She had seen the sea as placid as a baby's bath or angry and punishing in the midst of a hurricane. Sometimes it seemed as if all the answers to life's weighty questions resided in that enormous expanse of water.

Tonight, though, she sought a more human connection. She loved her brother dearly, but she wondered if he could be objective under the circumstances.

"Jonathan?"

"Hmm?" Her brother was lost in thought, his expression serious.

"Do you trust J.B.?"

Jonathan's head whipped around, his gaze incredulous. "He's my best friend. What kind of question is that? Of course I trust him. Surely you're not worried he's going to stiff you on this business deal. Is that why you're dragging your feet?"

"No, it's not that. I know he'll make me a fair offer. He already has, in fact. The only reason I haven't committed yet is because I wanted him to swing in the wind for a little while. The man is so damned arrogant. I couldn't stand the thought of giving in to him so easily."

Jonathan chuckled. "Well, he *is* arrogant, I'll grant you that. But he comes by it honestly. Everything he touches turns to gold."

"And on a personal level?"

"He and I have never done business together."

"That's not what I meant."

Jonathan stopped and faced her. "You're talking about women." He said it flatly. A statement. Not a question.

"I suppose I am."

"J.B. and I are grown men. We don't share locker room stories. What are you asking me, Mazie?"

She wrapped her arms around herself, feeling a chill now that they had stopped and their blood was cooling. "I'm not sure. I'm wondering what you know about his private life."

"As much as anybody, I guess." He started walking again, leaving Mazie to scamper in his wake to catch up. "He likes variety."

Her heart sank. She had come to the same conclusion. "Yeah…"

"Where's this coming from, sis?"

"He's asked me out on a date."

She threw it out there bluntly. No frills. Wondering what Jonathan would make of it.

For the second time, her brother ground to a halt. This time, his expression was thunderous. "Are you serious? I thought you hated the guy."

"Hate is a strong word. It seems like a bad idea, doesn't it?"

Jonathan made a motion with his hand. "Let's turn around." He walked in silence for a few moments. "Why ask me?"

"Well…" She shrugged. "You and I both agree he flits from one woman to the next. If he and I get something going and then it's over, everything will be awkward. Especially for you."

"Do you *want* to go out with him, Mazie?"

Ah, there was the question. She took a deep breath, inhaling the scents of salt air and somewhere in the distance, meat sizzling on a grill. "I do. Even knowing it's probably self-destructive. I like him. A lot. But J.B. has always been our *friend*. It's weird for me."

"How do you think I feel?"

Her brother's wry comment made her smile. "Well, don't worry. It will probably be a one-time thing. I can't imagine that he and I have what it takes to be a couple." Even talking about it sounded bizarre. There was a very good chance the *date* was an attempt to butter her up.

"Don't sell yourself short. J.B. isn't *only* a successful businessman. He does have a life."

"Unlike you," she said, suddenly eager to change the subject.

"Don't start on me, Mazie. Work has been hell lately. Dad goes in every day and creates messes I have to undo. And then I still have *my* projects to deal with. I don't know how much longer we can keep going like this."

"Is it time for him to step down?"

"I think so, yes. But how do I tell him that?"

"What about Hartley? Couldn't he help you?"

Jonathan's low curse shocked her. It was totally unlike him.

His voice was tense and angry. "There is no Hartley," he said. "He's not coming back. And even if he did, it wouldn't matter. Dad has cut him out of the will."

Sick dismay rolled through her chest. "But why?"

"I can't tell you. Or I don't want to tell you," he said, his voice weary. "He's your brother. I don't want to ruin your illusions. But trust me when I say there are some sins a man commits that are unforgivable."

"But I—"

He cut her off with a sharp slash of his hand. "I won't talk to you about this, Mazie. I love you dearly, but the subject is closed."

Jonathan's vehement tone ended the conversation. Their peaceful walk was ruined.

Tears stung her eyes. Jonathan complained about chaos at the shipping company, but for Mazie, All That Glitters was the stability in her life. At home she had a rapidly declining parent, one brother who was working himself to death and another who had apparently abandoned them all. Even worse—though he didn't say much about it—Jonathan's headaches were increasingly severe. It worried her.

They were almost back to the house. She touched his arm. "I'm sorry. I know you're carrying the business. I wish I could help."

He put an arm around her waist and hugged her. "It will all work out. It always does."

She sighed. "I feel like I should head up to Vermont to see Mama…sometime in the next two weeks."

Jonathan stopped. He rolled his shoulders. "I'm not ready to go inside yet."

They dropped down onto the sand. Mazie linked her arms around her knees. "I'll feel guilty if I don't make the effort."

"She doesn't even know who we are. Hasn't for years."

"I know. But she's my mother. And it's Christmas."

"We were there a month ago."

"Yes." The two of them had flown up to Stowe for a ski trip with friends. Afterward, they had stayed over a day, rented a car and driven to a tiny town near the New Hampshire border to make the sad, difficult visit.

"Have you ever wondered," Mazie said, "why Daddy found a place so damned far away from Charleston?"

Jonathan laughed, but there was no humor in it. "Oh, yeah. To his credit, Ravenwood is tops in the nation for residential care facilities. Believe me, I've checked. So no one can fault him there. He's paying a king's ransom to keep her in safety and comfort."

"But my cynical side tells me he doesn't want to have to think about her. It's easier if she's a thousand miles away."

"That about sums it up."

"When was the last time he went up there?"

"I'm not sure. Two years ago. Three?"

"He could have divorced her."

"I think he probably still loves her, Mazie."

She winced inwardly. Maybe the Tarletons were

every one cursed…doomed to give their hearts un-
wisely. After all, wasn't Mazie contemplating doing
the same thing? She knew how J.B. had treated her in
the past, yet she was still hoping against hope that he
had changed.

They sat there in silence, listening to the crashing
waves, noting how exponentially many more stars there
were the longer they let their eyes adjust to the darkness.

She rested her chin on her knees. "I used to wish
we were a family like the Vaughans. Normal. Ordinary. Together."

Jonathan tousled her hair. "I'm not sure I'd call my
buddy ordinary, but yeah. I get your point." He leaned
back on his hands. "I guess we're all a little screwed up
because of what happened. I hated it for you the worst.
I remember the day Mom left you cried for hours."

"And you skipped baseball practice so you could
come home, sit on my bed and read *Little House on
the Prairie* to me."

"She wasn't much of a mom even when she still
lived with us. We pretty much raised ourselves."

"I know. It used to scare me when she would sit in
front of the window for hours on end and not speak."

"Don't go to Vermont, Mazie. It will make you too
sad. Wait until January, and I'll go with you. Or maybe
February."

"I'll think about it."

"And J.B.?"

She stood up and dusted the sand from her pants.
"I'll think about him, too. Who knows, Jonathan?
Maybe you and I are both too messed up to have seri-
ous relationships with anyone."

He rolled to his feet and shook himself like a dog. "Speak for yourself. I plan to get laid this weekend on a tropical island with a drink in one hand and sunscreen in the other."

"Really?"

He headed toward the gate, his laughter dancing on the breeze. "You're too gullible, Mazie Jane. I'd work on that before you go out with J.B."

Mazie gulped her coffee, burned her tongue and said an unladylike word. "Can you unlock the door? I don't know what I did with my keys."

Gina scooted past her, punched in the alarm code and wrestled with the cantankerous lock. "I hope we do move. I hate this door."

The two of them entered the shop and dumped their things in the back office. Mazie was usually the bubbly one in the mornings. Gina was slower to wake up. But Mazie had spent a restless night tossing and turning and wondering if she had the guts to call J.B. and cancel.

She didn't know which was worse. Going, or not going.

Now she was exhausted *and* conflicted.

Gina sifted through the mail she had picked up from their postal box. "Two bills, an invitation to a reception at the Gullah Cultural Center and seven catalogs. Maybe *we* should consider doing a catalog. The bulk mailings must produce business, or we wouldn't be drowning under the weight of them."

"It's even worse at home. The recycle bin overflows this time of year."

"Look at this one," Gina said. "It's an English company that sells organic scented soaps. Their packaging is really nice. We could add some little things like that to put pops of color in the shop. Even jewelry can get monotonous when it's all gold and silver."

"Bite your tongue," Mazie said, laughing.

As they ran through their morning rituals, Mazie felt the strongest urge to tell Gina everything that had happened in the bank vault, and then last night on the veranda. She needed advice. Support. A dose of impartial sanity.

She was supposed to be planning her revenge, not thinking about how good it felt to kiss J.B. To touch him. To feel his hands on her body.

Gina waved a hand in front of Mazie's face. "Hellooo… you spaced out on me, boss. I need you to focus. We've got not one, but two cruise ships today. And it's Friday, so the Holiday Weekends festival starts. We're going to be run ragged."

"You're right."

Gina cocked her head. "Are you okay, Mazie?"

Seven

Mazie changed the subject and busied herself unwrapping a shipment of earrings.

As the afternoon passed, one thought kept spinning in her brain. She wasn't going to sleep with J.B. Of course she wasn't.

But the whole time she was getting ready after work that afternoon, she couldn't help wondering if he was contemplating taking her home with him after dinner. Given what had transpired in the bank vault, it wasn't an entirely out-in-left-field idea. Clearly he knew that going back to *her* place was out of the question.

She left the shop at three in order to get a mani-pedi before going home. Tonight's encounter required all the confidence she could muster. Whether the evening turned out to be business or pleasure or both, she had to be prepared, mentally and physically.

Fortunately, her wardrobe wasn't a problem. A year ago, for a black-tie charity gala, she had ordered a beautiful holiday dress from an online catalog. At the last minute, she had come down with a twenty-four-hour bug and didn't get to attend the event. The gown had been hanging in her closet ever since.

It wasn't really the kind of thing she could use during another season of the year. The floor-length dress was deep green velvet. The fabric was elegant and classic, the design even more so. A plunging neckline showcased her breasts. The back of the dress also dipped in a deep vee, leaving her arms and shoulders bare.

She debated longer over her hair than anything else. If it were summer, she would put it up, no question. But the weather was perfect today, and with all that bare skin showing, maybe having her hair down around her shoulders was a good idea.

Fortunately for her nerves, Jonathan hadn't yet returned from the office when it was time for J.B. to arrive. Her father was out of the house also, having dinner with friends. Mazie had said goodbye to him earlier as he left with his driver.

Mazie sent the cook and housekeeper home early, so when J.B. pulled up in front of the house in his luxury SUV, no one was around to witness the moment. She peeked out and watched him lope up the front stairs.

He was a gorgeous man, beautiful enough to make her breath catch in her throat. J.B. would hate being called *beautiful*, but the adjective fit. Though his features weren't perfectly symmetrical, and he didn't have the kind of slick sophistication of a model, there was something intensely masculine about him.

He was a chameleon, really.

In a business setting, she had seen him play the part of the successful entrepreneur, both charming and hard-dealing. But when J.B. and Jonathan headed out to North Carolina to camp in the mountains or took off on a weeklong cruise down the coast in J.B.'s sailboat, his tanned limbs and casual clothing made him look like a rugged outdoorsman.

She took one last quick peek before opening the door.

Tonight, in a classic black tuxedo and crisp white shirt, he was a heartbreaker. Mazie knew that side of him better than most.

J.B. was stunned to find that he was nervous as hell. When Mazie opened the door, his heart slugged hard in his chest. Her glorious chestnut hair spilled across her shoulders, thick and wavy. The green dress she wore showcased her slender figure. His fingers itched to stroke all that soft fabric.

But his sense of self-preservation sounded an alarm.

Instead of touching her, he cleared his throat and smiled. "You look stunning, Mazie. I've got the heat running in the car, in case you don't want to bother with a wrap. It's not really all that cold tonight. You could always throw a coat in the back seat for later."

She had stepped back to allow him to enter. Now he stood in the foyer, wanting to sweep her up in his arms and kiss her senseless. Instead, he jammed his hands in his pockets and practiced self-control.

Mazie's smile was guarded. "Thank you. I'll do that."

The current atmosphere could best be described as wary. The physical awareness between them was on a slow boil, but because he had hurt her once, she didn't trust him. He'd have to work on that.

It took Mazie only a matter of moments to lock the door and set the alarm. When she was done, he put a hand beneath her elbow and steadied her as they descended the stairs. The minimal physical contact was enough to make his blood heat.

He helped her into the front seat before closing the door. Then he ran around to the driver's side. As he had promised, the car was toasty warm.

Mazie buckled her seat belt and folded her hands in her lap, her spine straight. It wasn't the posture of a woman prepared to enjoy an exciting evening. If anything, she seemed to be braced for unpleasant news.

"I don't bite," he said teasingly.

They exited the main gates, and he steered the car toward the Ravenel Bridge.

She shot him a sideways glance. "I'm not sure this was a good idea," she said. "We have nothing in common."

Her tone was prissy enough to annoy him. "It didn't seem that way when you locked us in that bank vault."

"That was an accident."

"So you say." He loved teasing her. "We have history, Mazie."

"I'm surprised you'd want to bring that up."

Bingo. Now he knew for sure what land mines lay in his path. She was pissed, even now, about him turning her down years ago.

"You're still mad about that prom thing?"

"Don't flatter yourself." Her fingers made patterns in the velvet. "I got over my embarrassing crush pretty quickly after that night. You were an arrogant jerk.

And unkind on top of that. But I learned from that experience."

"Learned what?"

"Not to trust you."

He flinched inwardly. There were extenuating circumstances, explanations that could clear his name, but he wasn't the only person involved, and he didn't want to cause a rift between her and Jonathan. Even now, J.B.'s behavior was risky. It was the reason he had kept his distance for years.

"I'd like to propose a truce," he said lightly, his fingers clenched on the steering wheel. "What if we start over? A new relationship. A new beginning." He told himself he needed her goodwill so she would sell him her property. Surely he wasn't really considering something so much more unpredictable.

"Why would we do that?"

"It's the season of peace and goodwill. Isn't that enough?" He reached across the small distance separating them and touched her wrist. "This isn't about me stealing your property, Mazie. I want it, yes. But we can do business another day. Tonight, I'm only interested in *you*."

He hadn't meant to be so honest, but her inability to accept him at face value was frustrating.

At the hotel, J.B. handed off his keys with a large tip, large enough to guarantee he'd get the car back with no dings or scratches.

The front door was only steps away. He glanced at his passenger. "Do you want to keep your coat?"

"No. I'm fine."

The seat of the SUV was high. Mazie's legs were long, but her dress was fitted. Without asking permission, he put his hands on her waist and lifted her down to the narrow red carpet that led to the entrance.

Overhead, a canvas awning protected them from nonexistent rain. Huge concrete urns on either side overflowed with holly and magnolia blossoms and burgundy satin ribbons.

Mazie's face lit up, her reserve melting in the festive atmosphere. "This is lovely." She actually squeezed his hand momentarily, leaving him to grin like a kid who'd just gotten a gold star for a perfect spelling test. Unfortunately, the moment was far too short.

He curled an arm around her waist and ushered her inside.

Étoile de Mer was old Charleston at her finest. Five years ago, the series of narrow buildings tucked away on a side street had been an aging inn past its prime with a different name. But new owners had completely renovated the connected eighteenth-century row houses.

The result was a chic, luxurious boutique hotel that catered to travelers with the means to splurge, whether that be millennials or baby boomers. The main floor of the hotel included a bar and lounge along with a five-star restaurant that was booked for six months in advance.

J.B. had called in a few favors, made a handful of promises and wrangled a prime reservation for seven o'clock.

Seeing the expression on Mazie's face was worth every bit of hassle.

The host led them up a shallow flight of stairs to the mezzanine level. Their table was tucked inside a bay window overlooking the street.

Once they had ordered an appetizer and wine, J.B. leaned back in his chair and studied his companion. "Have you eaten here before?"

Mazie shook her head. "No. I do go out with friends often, but we generally pick something more casual. And my social life isn't nonstop. Jonathan and I take turns looking after Dad when we want to be gone overnight."

"He can't be on his own?"

"Oh, he could be," Mazie said. "But Jonathan and I are his emotional crutches. Once Hartley disappeared, I think Daddy gave up and started thinking like an old man."

"Do you know where your brother is?"

Mazie shook her head, her expression bleak. "No. I don't even know what happened. Jonathan won't tell me. Do *you* know?"

J.B. shook his head. "Sorry. No idea. Jonathan and I are tight, but he hasn't said much at all about Hartley."

"Oh." She sighed. "I was hoping you could clue me in. The whole thing is frightening. To be honest, it hurts. He and I were very close. I can't believe he left without saying a word." Mazie traced a pattern in the condensation on her water glass with her fingertip. "I used to be terribly jealous of your family," she said. Her rueful sideways glance told him she wasn't kidding.

"Really? Why?"

"The Vaughans are all so incredibly normal. I never had normal in my life. You're lucky, J.B."

The comment caught him off guard. "I suppose I am," he said. The waiter interrupted the conversation, arriving to take their order. Mazie chose shrimp étouffée on a bed of fluffy rice. J.B. asked for the rare filet topped with a crabmeat garnish.

When they were alone again, he picked up the threads of the conversation. "What happens to your father when you or Jonathan decide to get married?"

Mazie wrinkled her nose. "I don't know that either of us has to worry about that. My dear brother doesn't let himself get close to anyone, and I'm…" She trailed off, looking uncomfortable.

"You're what?"

"Scared." She tossed the word at him with an almost visible chip on her shoulder.

"Scared of what?"

"I don't want to love someone so much that it blinds me or traps me. My parents are hardly a shining example of marital success. You know the statistics. You've lived them. No offense."

He winced inwardly. Mazie had faced more than her share of abandonment. She must surely have been conflicted about her father sending her mother away, no matter the circumstances.

"I hear what you're saying, but I'm not sure your argument holds water, though. I had the greatest example of marriage in the world, and still I got duped by a money hungry social climber who ruined my credit and cleaned out my bank accounts in the divorce."

"Did your parents try to stop you?"

"Of course they did. Several friends weighed in, too, Jonathan included. But I was blinded by physical infatuation." Wasn't that what he risked now?

"Not too blind to see what you were getting out of the arrangement."

Mazie's humor soothed old wounds. "I was twenty-two years old and driven by my hormones. It wasn't my finest hour."

"To be honest, I was away at college most of that year, so I didn't hear more than the occasional flurry of gossip. But I remember being very surprised."

He cocked his head. "Why?"

"Because you were always so sure of what you wanted. At the risk of pumping up your already enormous ego, I couldn't imagine any woman walking away from you after only a few months, even if you *were* difficult to live with. Maybe she had the money thing planned from the start."

"If you're trying to make me feel better, it's not working."

Her grin was impish. "Sorry. I've known you and hated you for too long to tiptoe around your feelings... always assuming you *have* feelings." The smile told him she was making a joke at his expense. She wasn't trying to impress him, that was for sure.

"I have feelings," he said, deadpan. "I'm having a feeling right now." He flirted deliberately, for nothing more than the sheer pleasure of watching her react.

Mazie didn't seem to know what to make of him.

She concentrated on her food, most likely disconcerted by his deliberately intimate teasing. When at last she lifted her head and pinned him with an amber-eyed gaze, he knew in an instant that he had waded into deep water.

"Let me ask you something, J.B.," she said.

He waved a hand. "Anything at all. I'm an open book."

"If we hadn't gotten locked in the bank vault and

ended up in an extremely compromising position, would you ever have considered asking me out?"

His fork was halfway to his mouth. The bite of tender beef went untasted. Slowly, he set down the utensil, dabbed his lips with a snowy napkin and frowned. "I feel like this is one of those questions women throw out to trip a guy up."

"It's no trick. I'm merely asking—would we be sitting here right now if you didn't have claustrophobia, and we didn't use sex to take your mind off the fact that we were trapped? You've had a decade to ask me out on a date. Why now?"

Mazie watched J.B.'s face, zeroing in on every nuance of expression. She'd like to think her intuition could spot any dissembling on his part. Then again, the man was a practiced charmer. Girls had been throwing themselves at him since he was in middle school.

It was no wonder he was so confident he could acquire her property. He was accustomed to the dominoes always falling his way. The world cooperated with J.B. Inevitably.

While it was true that his youthful marriage had been a bad misstep, he had survived. He'd been humiliated and chastened and perhaps, at the time, even heartbroken. Still, it seemed unlikely he had suffered any lasting damage.

His silence in the aftermath of her question was ominous. Was he inventing a pretty story? Concocting a tale that would flatter her and woo her?

"J.B.?"

He shook his head. "You ask difficult questions,

Mazie Tarleton. Maybe I wanted to be sure I was giving you a thoughtful response. Maybe I needed to comb through my own motives. Maybe I'm not even sure why I invited you to dinner. Or maybe I was afraid the truth would make you angry."

She gaped at him, unprepared for this level of transparency. "So what did you come up with? Don't keep me in suspense."

While she waited, breathless, needing to hear what J.B. had to say, their waiter arrived with the main courses. Though the food looked and smelled amazing, Mazie wanted to banish the poor man to the kitchen. J.B. had been hovering on the verge of complete honesty. She wanted desperately to hear his response.

Instead, she had to be content with a seemingly endless parade of servers and sommeliers and even the manager who wanted to make sure every single thing about the dinner was to their liking.

By the time the two of them were finally alone again, the moment had passed.

Mazie sighed inwardly. An orchestra on the level below them had begun playing a medley of familiar Christmas songs. The restaurant buzzed with laughter and the clinking of crystal.

On any other occasion and with any other companion, Mazie would be basking in a haze of warm contentment.

Instead, she ate her meal automatically. All she could think about was the man sitting across from her. Why was he stalling?

He poured each of them another glass of wine, finished his steak and then stared at her.

"The answer is no," he said. "I wouldn't have. The reason I asked you out has *everything* to do with what happened in the bank vault."

Eight

Mazie froze, sensing danger. J.B.'s eyes were dark… intense. More navy blue tonight than royal. And nothing about him suggested lighthearted teasing.

She swallowed, her throat suddenly as dry as sandpaper. "I see."

He drank recklessly, the muscles in his throat rippling as he swallowed. Without warning, some line had been crossed, some barrier breached.

Gone was the good-natured, sophisticated businessman. The wealthy entrepreneur.

In his place was a primal male with flushed cheekbones, glittering sapphire eyes, and a big body that radiated warmth and raw masculinity.

In his right hand, he held a crystal goblet. His left hand moved restlessly on the white linen tablecloth. Against the pristine fabric, his tanned fingers drummed a rhythm only he could hear.

At last he stared at her moodily, his brows dark, his mood volatile. "Is that all you have to say?"

"I may have given you the wrong impression about me," she whispered, conscious of people coming and going nearby.

"Or maybe you hide the real you from the world."

"I'm not that kind of woman," she said desperately. "It was the adrenaline or something."

"Or something…" He laughed without humor. "You're a sensual woman, Mazie. Sexy and beautiful and damned appealing in every way. We've been dancing around each other for years, always careful never to get too close. I've seen you move across a crowded room to avoid me. Why?"

"You're imagining things," she said, aghast that he had noticed. But of course he had. The man never missed anything. She'd been protecting herself, plain and simple. And he had known, damn him.

"No." His rebuttal was flat. Certain. "I'm not imagining *anything*. You've kept the width of this city between us, but yesterday when I had my embarrassing meltdown, your compassion was stronger than your need to keep your distance. When we touched, it was gasoline on a fire."

"Please don't say things like that," she begged. "It isn't true."

"You can deny it all you like, but I was there, Mazie. So yes…that's why I asked you out. Even though I knew it was a bad idea. I couldn't wait to touch you again." He stood and tossed his napkin on the table. "Dance with me, sweet girl. Dessert will keep."

His hand closed around her wrist. Gently, inexorably, he drew her to her feet.

Mazie trembled. It was impossible to meet his gaze. Not now. Not when her heart slammed against her ribs and her breasts ached for his touch.

He led her down the carpeted stairs and into the salon where a polished dance floor stretched from wall to wall. Overhead, a phalanx of miniature crystal chandeliers, draped in mistletoe and bows, cast a rainbow of shimmering light over the dancers.

The room wasn't large. J.B. pulled her into his arms and held her tightly. They fell into the music as one, barely missing a note or a step. Some men hated dancing. J.B. moved as if he knew the music by heart.

She felt cosseted in his embrace, but at the same time shiveringly aware of the shark-infested waters that might lie ahead. Already her body responded to his caress. His heart beat a steady rhythm beneath her palm. His fingers were warm on the bare skin of her lower back. They didn't speak.

Words weren't necessary.

It wasn't her imagination that other women sneaked peeks at the man who held her so carefully. His breath was warm at her temple. The scent of his crisply starched shirt teased her nostrils.

Her body warmed and melted into his. They were in a very public venue. Dancing was the only acceptable, legitimate reason for a man and woman to be so close.

One song segued into the next. Mazie knew every word, every chorus. For so many Christmases she had wondered about her future. For so many Christmases, she had told herself she despised J.B.

Now the whole world was changing.

She could have danced all night. Her feet barely noticed the pain in her toes, the strain in her calves. For a woman who spent her days in flats or athletic shoes, tonight's escapade was a dose of reality.

Being glamorous hurt.

At last, J.B. was the one to call a halt. He brushed a strand of hair from her hot cheek. "How about a drink?" The words were commonplace. The look in his eyes, anything but.

She nodded, flushed with a confusing mixture of excitement and dread. Whatever happened tonight was up to her. No matter how many times she told herself she had to stay away from J.B., the truth was far simpler.

He was her kryptonite.

She wanted him.

Hand in hand, they ascended the stairs to their intimate table for two. Dessert menus appeared. She downed two glasses of ice water. Her wineglass was refilled, as if by magic.

When their caramel-laced bread pudding arrived, Mazie shook her head. "I don't think I can. I'm stuffed."

J.B.'s heavy-lidded gaze never left her face. "A taste at least," he coaxed. He scooped up a bite. It was covered in whipped cream.

Mazie opened her mouth automatically when he held out the spoon. Her thighs clenched beneath the table. "Yum," she mumbled, chewing and swallowing.

The man was a devil. She wanted to strip him out of that tux and do naughty things to his body.

His slight smile told her he knew exactly what thoughts were running through her head. Without warning, he leaned forward and kissed the edge of her mouth, his tongue delicately swiping a residue of sweet cream. "You taste delectable."

"Stop," she said, breathing hard. "People are watching."

"It was barely a kiss. Don't worry. No one can see."

She realized he was right. The restaurant lights had been dimmed. A trio of short red candles flickered on their table. With the antique privacy screens and artfully placed foliage, Mazie and J.B. were in a world of their own.

The waiter still stopped by, of course, but not as often now that dinner was almost done.

She sipped her wine, awash in a haze of incredulity. Not only was she enjoying herself, but she was spending time with J.B., and she didn't want to kill him. That was progress, right?

Fortunately for her emotional equilibrium, he didn't try to feed her any more dessert. She ate another couple of bites and left it to him to finish. The man was tall and athletic. He could afford the calories.

While they were dancing, J.B. had left his cell phone on the table, silenced of course. Suddenly, it vibrated. He glanced at it automatically, and before he could say anything, another call came in from the same number.

"It's my sister Leila," he said. "She never calls this time of day. Will you excuse me, Mazie?"

"Of course."

As he stood, the phone buzzed a third time.

Something told her it wasn't good news. As she watched, J.B. hurried down the stairs and out the front door where he could talk in private. Though she was at the window, she couldn't see him on the street.

Less than five minutes later, he returned, his face white beneath his tan. "I'm so sorry," he said. "But I have to go. It's my mother." He swallowed hard. "She's had a massive heart attack. They don't know the damage yet. She may have to have surgery tonight."

Mazie's eyes widened. J.B.'s family was close. The matriarch was beloved. "Go," she said, waving her hand at him. "I'll take care of the bill and grab a taxi. Go. Hurry." She lifted a hand and summoned the waiter.

J.B. hesitated, his usual expression robbed of its suave confidence. "I hate to leave you."

She jumped off the emotional deep end. "I could come with you." Even strong men needed support occasionally.

The waiter handed over the check. J.B. pulled out his credit card. When the man walked away, J.B. looked at her and sighed. "I'd like that. If you're sure you want to."

Were both of them thinking about what they were giving up tonight? "Will it seem odd to your family if I show up with you?"

"You know them all. Nobody will notice."

That was debatable.

The waiter dropped off the bill. J.B. scribbled his name and pocketed his credit card. And they were done.

The valet brought the car in record time. J.B. handed over another generous tip and tucked Mazie into the front seat.

She was hardly dressed for a hospital visit. Neither was he.

J.B. drove the maze of downtown streets with a reckless intensity that was only slightly alarming. At the hospital, he screeched into a parking spot in the emergency room lot and hopped out, pausing to help Mazie.

"I can wait in the car," she said, feeling conspicuous in her fancy dress.

He gripped her wrist. "I want you to come."

Once they were inside, it was only a matter of moments until a nurse directed them to the appropriate cubicle. The heart surgeon had just arrived to talk to the family. They were standing in the hall, though Mazie could see J.B.'s mother through the partially open door. The older woman was hooked up to a multitude of machines.

Most families would probably be scolded for having too many visitors. Since the Vaughans had outfitted an entire pediatric wing in recent years, they were VIPs.

The man's face was grave. "Mrs. Vaughan suffered a very dangerous cardiac event. She is weak and not entirely stable. I don't think we should wait until morning for the surgery."

Mazie recognized J.B.'s father and his two sisters, Leila and Alana. As children, Mazie and Jonathan and Hartley had spent large amounts of time at the Vaughan home. But it had been years since she had been close to them as a friend.

Both of J.B.'s sisters had red-rimmed eyes. His father looked exhausted and stressed. Mr. Vaughan nodded. "We're in your hands, Dr. Pritchard. Tell us what to do."

The doctor made a note on his clipboard. "She's been asking for her son." He looked at J.B. "Once you've had a chance to spend a few minutes with her, we'll prep her for surgery." He paused, grimacing. "I don't want to alarm you unnecessarily, but I need you to know that the surgery carries significant risk. Without it, she'll suffer another heart attack, possibly fatal. So we don't really have a choice."

Mr. Vaughan spoke up, his eyes sunken and underscored with shadows. "You're saying that her other health conditions make it complicated."

The doctor nodded. "Yes. Her autoimmune disease and the high blood pressure are problematic." He looked at all of them. "We need her to fight and to believe she is going to be okay. So no crying, no drama."

J.B.'s expression was grim, his jaw taut. "Understood."

"If you'll excuse me," the doctor said, "I'll go make sure the OR is being prepped. Once the surgery begins, we'll keep you posted in the surgical waiting lounge." With a brief nod, he disappeared down the hall.

J.B. squared his shoulders. "I'll talk to her," he said.

His father hugged him tightly. "We can't lose her, son. She's the center of this family. She's our rock."

"I know, Dad. I know."

J.B. shot Mazie a look she couldn't read. He hugged his sisters. Then he stepped through the door. "Hey, Mom. What's this I hear about you scaring Dad? That's not nice."

The four people left standing in the hallway strained to hear.

Mrs. Vaughan's expression brightened when she saw her firstborn. "Don't you look handsome. A date tonight?"

"Yes, Mama."

"That's nice."

Tears stung Mazie's eyes when J.B. perched on the edge of the bed and carefully took his mother's hand in both of his. He kissed her fingers. "You gave us a scare, but you're going to be fine."

His mother's wrinkled nose and half frown told Mazie that the woman was well aware of her situation.

"I want you to promise me something, sweetheart." Her voice was hoarse and weak.

J.B. nodded. "Whatever you need, Mom. You name it."

"If anything happens to me, I want you to take care of your dad and your sisters. They will depend on you, J.B."

Leila moaned and burst into tears, though she muffled her sobs and moved away from the door. Alana curled an arm around her father's waist.

Mazie's eyes were damp, as well.

Through the door, she saw J.B. lean down and kiss his mother's cheek. "We're not going to talk like that. I have a surprise for you. I was going to wait until Christmas to tell everybody, but you should know tonight. I've asked Mazie Tarleton to marry me. We're engaged. And the good Lord willing, she and I won't wait too long to get started on those grandchildren you've always wanted."

Mrs. Vaughan's face lit up, and a tear rolled down her cheek. "Really, son? Oh, that's wonderful."

Mazie was stunned for thirty seconds until she realized what J.B. was doing. He was giving his mother a reason to fight, a reason to live. Mazie expected the three Vaughans in the hallway to give her the third degree, but they were too focused on what was happening in the emergency room cubicle.

She sucked in a sharp breath. For a moment, J.B.'s playacting hit a nerve. If she really hated the man, why did his pretend words reach deep inside her and squeeze her heart?

Mrs. Vaughan peered around her son. "Is she here, J.B.? I haven't seen her in ages."

J.B. looked over his shoulder, his gaze clashing with Mazie's. She nodded slowly, alarmed by how appealing it was to play this unexpected role. Had she honestly blinded herself to the truth so completely? Did she want to be J.B.'s fiancée, even as part of a benevolent lie?

Heaven help her. It felt wrong, but what could she do?

Mr. Vaughan and the two girls stepped aside. Mazie smoothed her skirt. She was still holding her small evening purse. She passed it off to Alana and eased the door open. "I'm here, Mrs. Vaughan."

J.B.'s mother held out her hand. "Come sit where I can look at you. And call me Jane. Oh, honey, you're stunning. That dress makes you look like a model. I know your mother would be so proud."

J.B. stood up so Mazie could take his place. She sat down on the bed gingerly, not wanting to disturb any of the medical equipment. "I haven't seen you in forever, Mrs. Vaughan. Jane, I mean. I'm so sorry you've been ill."

Jane Vaughan beamed, her hand touching the soft velvet of Mazie's skirt. "I couldn't be happier," she said. "Let me see the ring." She reached for Mazie's left hand.

Mazie curled her fingers defensively. "J.B. wanted me to help pick out the ring. So we don't have it yet."

J.B. moved closer. He rested a hand on Mazie's shoulder. His fingers were warm on the bare skin at the curve of her neck. "I won't make her wait long, Mom. This just happened."

"I see."

For a moment it seemed as though J.B.'s mother saw through their subterfuge. But her smile didn't waver.

J.B. hugged Mazie and then leaned down to brush his lips across his mother's brow. "When you're on the mend, we'd like your help with wedding plans."

"Oh, yes," Mazie said. "You know all the venues in Charleston and all the best vendors. I'll need all the backup I can get."

Jane was misty-eyed. She gripped her son's hand… and Mazie's. "I wouldn't miss this wedding for the world."

J.B. chuckled. "Consider it good practice for when Leila and Alana tie the knot."

Mazie stood, keenly aware of the warmth of J.B.'s big frame at her back. "I'll let you rest now."

J.B. nodded. "I love you, Mama. And I'll be here during the surgery. We all will. Don't be afraid."

Jane smiled weakly, obviously tired out by the conversation. "I'm not scared. Your father and I have lived a good life. If it's my time to go, don't let him be sad."

Mazie leaned down and kissed her cheek, realizing how much she had missed having a maternal role model as she reached adulthood. "You can't go," she said firmly. "We all need you."

As she slipped out of the room, the others came in to say their last words of encouragement. The nurse arrived with pre-op sedation.

Mazie leaned against the wall in the hallway and said a prayer for Jane's safety.

When J.B. exited the room, he eyed her warily. Unspoken feelings simmered between them.

She shook her head in bemusement. "You always did think fast on your feet." It wasn't really a compliment.

He scraped his hands through his hair. "I don't mean to make light of marriage, but I wanted her to have a reason to fight."

"Of course you did. But the rest of your family?"

"Let's keep the truth to ourselves for now. Explaining the ruse is unnecessary. They have enough on their plate."

This lie might keep her tied to him indefinitely. She wasn't sure how she felt about that. "I'm going to call a cab," she said quietly.

"I'll drive you home."

"No. You need to be here. I'll be fine." The J.B. she knew had disappeared. In his place, she saw a man who was worried and trying not to show it.

She was getting in too deep. She didn't want to admire him or feel sympathy for him. Her years-long antipathy was the only thing protecting her from doing something stupid.

No one would blame her if she ran far and fast. Getting too close to J.B. threatened her hard-won composure.

For a decade and more she had convinced herself that she didn't even like the man. How could her feelings have changed so radically? Her heart pounded. *Walk away, Mazie. Walk away.* Despite her best intentions, emotionally charged words tumbled from her lips. Words that said her heart was far more involved than she was prepared to admit. "Would you like to me to come back after I change clothes?"

Nine

J.B. looked stunned. Somehow the lie he had spouted was changing everything. This felt intimate. Emotionally charged. She found herself offering help and comfort as if she were a real fiancée.

He nodded slowly, his gaze unguarded for a surprising moment. "Yes, please."

"Do you want me to go by your place and bring you something else to wear?" She knew where he lived. She and Jonathan and Hartley had been to parties there. It was a fabulous home overlooking the Battery.

"You don't mind?" He seemed to be weighing his words as if afraid of spooking her.

"Not at all. I'll call Jonathan and tell him what's going on so Dad won't worry."

He nodded. "I'll text you the alarm code and what to grab for me." When he handed her his keys and their fingers brushed, his touch burned. "Do you feel comfortable driving the SUV?" he asked.

"Not entirely, but I'll take it slow. It's late. There won't be much traffic."

He cupped her chin in his hand. "Thanks, Mazie. I never expected the evening to end this way."

He kissed her softly. At first, it was a kiss of gratitude...of kinship. But in a flash it went somewhere far darker. It seduced her, cajoled her and made her heart beat faster.

His lips were firm and demanding, his smothered groan telling her that the reluctant connection between them, the one neither of them really wanted or needed, was not easy to eradicate.

This wasn't how they had anticipated the evening would end.

She pulled away. "I should go."

Having J.B. look at her this way was alarming and disconcerting. They had moved from a romantic, flirtatious evening to something far more real.

He nodded, his gaze heavy with emotions she couldn't decipher. "Be careful. And call me if you have any problems."

"I'll be back as soon as I can." She touched his hand. "She'll pull through, J.B. She's a strong woman."

"I hope you're right."

Back at home, Mazie peeled out of the velvet dress with a wistful sigh. After changing into soft jeans and a lemon-yellow cotton sweater, she grabbed a canvas tote and stuffed it with water and snacks. There was no telling how long she would be with J.B. during his vigil.

Entering his home a short while later gave her an

odd feeling in the pit of her stomach. Though they had known each other for years, they were not on intimate terms. Or at least they hadn't been until the episode in the bank vault.

She walked through the elegant living room and dining room and climbed the stairs to the upper floor. J.B.'s bedroom commanded the best view in the house, not that she could see anything at this hour.

Though she had already accessed his text for the alarm code, now she checked again, making note of the items he wanted and where to find them. Pants, shirt, socks. A sweater. Casual shoes. A clean pair of boxers. Her cheeks heated. It was a good thing there was no one around to see her reaction.

In his closet she found the leather carry-all he had requested. She stuffed everything into it and took one last look at his text. These few items would hold him until he could come back home. A man didn't need to spend the night wearing a tux, even if it *was* hand-tailored just for him.

She stood in the center of his bedroom for a moment, making sure she hadn't forgotten anything. It was impossible not to look at his massive king-size bed. The wood was dark and heavy, the comforter crimson damask. How many women had J.B. entertained in this luxurious space?

Not her business. Not at all.

Ignoring her hot cheeks, she ran back downstairs, reset the alarm and scooted out the front door. This time, driving the huge SUV was not quite so intimidating.

When she made it back to the hospital, it was the middle of the night. The surgical waiting room was deserted except for the four Vaughans. J.B.'s two sisters were asleep, curled awkwardly on a duo of love seats. Mr. Vaughan was dozing also.

J.B. paced restlessly, looking darkly handsome despite his fatigue.

He greeted her quietly. "That was fast."

"There's no traffic at this hour." She held out the leather satchel. "Here you go. I know you must be ready to get out of that tux."

His sexy grin was a shadow of its usual wattage. "Is that an invitation, Mazie? I'll have to take a rain check."

She pretended his teasing didn't fluster her. "Try to behave. Is there any word yet?"

He yawned. "No. The surgery actually started thirty minutes ago. They said it could take hours."

"Go change," she said. "I'll wait right here."

Though J.B. in a tux was eye candy of the best kind, she almost preferred the man who returned moments later. A rumpled J.B. in casual clothes was dangerously appealing.

She raised an eyebrow. "Where's your tux?"

"I wadded it up in the bag. Has to go the cleaners anyway."

"Ah. Do you want to sit, or shall we walk the halls?"

"You're probably tired," he said.

"My adrenaline is still pumping. If you want to make a few laps of the building, I'm game."

J.B. poked his head into the lounge long enough leave his bag and to tell his dad where to find him. Then he rejoined Mazie. "Let's go. I can't stand to do nothing but wait."

J.B. was ridiculously glad to see Mazie.

He was a selfish bastard for asking her to stay, but

her presence gave him something to hang on to. In front of his sisters and his dad, he had to be strong and unflappable. With Mazie, he could be himself. The distinction should have worried him, but he was too tired to think about the reasons why.

For now, he would ignore his ambivalent reactions to being with her in this charged situation.

They walked the halls in silence. His name and his face were well-known in Charleston, particularly to the hospital staff. His family had been major benefactors for years.

No one bothered Mazie or him. A few nurses here and there said hello. With the lights dimmed and most patients asleep, the building was sleepy and secure.

He ignored the elevators and climbed the stairs, Mazie on his heels.

When they were both breathing hard, he pushed open the door on 4B and crooked a finger at her. "Let's take a look at the babies."

Though the nurse on the other side of the glass frowned, she didn't shoo them away. He could almost watch Mazie's heart melt into a puddle of maternal instinct when she scanned the row of clear plastic bassinets. "They're so tiny," she whispered. "How can they be so small?"

"We were all that little once upon a time."

She bumped his hip with hers. "Not you, surely. I can't even imagine it."

They stood there in silence. A third of the infants slept peacefully. Another third blinked and examined their surroundings with myopic interest. But it was the last third who demanded all the attention. They wailed and scrunched up their faces, making their displeasure known.

He shuddered. "How do new parents do it? You can't Google how to take care of a newborn."

"Sure you can. You can Google anything. Besides, you promised your mother grandchildren. You'd better get over your fear of babies in a hurry."

"Are you volunteering?" His heart squeezed at the thought of having a daughter who looked like Mazie.

"Heck, no." She chewed her bottom lip. "To be honest, I've always been afraid that I might turn out like my mother. I love the idea of kids, but parenting scares me."

"And what about marriage?"

"What about it?"

He sneaked a sideways look at her, noting how intently she studied the helpless infants. "I thought every woman wanted to get married. You didn't object to being my fake fiancée." Under the circumstances, maybe he hadn't given her a chance to protest.

"C'mon, J.B. You can't be serious. This is the twenty-first century. Women have lots of choices."

"That doesn't answer my question." He was inordinately interested in her answer.

She shrugged. "I don't know if I'll *get* married. Watching what my father went through…"

"Did he ever consider divorcing your mother?" Divorce was a painful subject for J.B. His failure still stung deeply.

"No. At least I don't think so. Jonathan thinks he's still in love with her after all these years. But he never goes to see her."

"Because she doesn't recognize him?"

"I guess that's the reason. It must be very painful."

J.B. glanced at his watch. When Mazie let down her guard with him, he actually thought the two of them might finally be able to heal the decade-old rift. But no matter how appealing that prospect was, their timing was off. "We've been gone a long time. I'd better get back to the cardiac floor."

When they reached the surgical lounge, a nurse had just come out of the OR with an update. The surgery was going well. It would be at least another hour and a half, and then recovery.

J.B. grimaced. He took Mazie's arm and drew her away from the others. "Go home," he said. "I shouldn't have asked you to stay." Her skin was smooth and warm beneath his fingertips. He had to resist the urge to stroke her.

"Don't be silly. I'm here. Relax, J.B. I've got nowhere else I need to be." Her smile seemed genuine, though still cautious perhaps.

"This isn't the evening I had planned," he said, his voice husky with fatigue and something else he was too tired to hide.

She cupped his cheek in her hand. "If you're talking about sex, we already took that off the table…remember?"

"Says who?"

His teasing wasn't up to its usual wicked voltage.

"Says me." She paused. "I enjoyed tonight," she said. "Dinner. Dancing. When you're not being a condescending jerk and breaking a girl's heart, you're a pretty nice guy."

Mazie hadn't meant to be so honest, but it was hard to hold a grudge at 3:00 a.m.

J.B.'s jaw was shadowed with dark stubble. His hair

was rumpled. The clothes she had brought him smelled of starch and laundry detergent. The blue button-up shirt and navy cotton pullover strained across his broad, hard chest.

The man looked like he had just crawled out of the covers and thrown on whatever was at hand. And yet he was still the sexiest thing she had ever seen.

She flashed back to his bedroom, for one brief moment imagining herself sprawled on that ruby comforter with J.B. leaning over her.

Her breathing quickened.

To make things worse, she couldn't help remembering the pink and blue swaddled babies. No matter what she'd said to JB, she *wanted* to have a normal family like his. But it just wasn't in the cards for her.

Even her own brother had disappeared.

The Tarletons were a mess.

J.B. took her arm. "Let's sit down. Are you hungry?"

"No," she said. They settled onto a padded bench. Once she was off her feet, the fatigue came crashing over.

He pulled her into his chest, wrapping an arm around her. "Close your eyes. Catnaps are my specialty."

The man wasn't kidding. In seconds he was snoring softly.

Mazie sighed and tried to do the same. But she couldn't relax. Being this close to J.B. lowered her defenses. She didn't *want* to like him. She didn't want to empathize about his worry for his mother. And she surely didn't want to be engaged to him.

Once upon a time, she would have welcomed the chance to be part of J.B.'s life. Those dreams had been crushed early and well. Now, she was almost positive that this sudden affability on his part was a calculated effort to win her trust.

The reality of selling her building to him was not the point. If she decided to go through with it, she would make him pay dearly for the privilege of relocating her.

No, what was really dangerous to her peace of mind was the possibility that J.B. could worm his way into her heart and then walk away when he got what he wanted.

While Mazie struggled internally with the extraordinary feeling of being wrapped in J.B.'s arms, Leila awakened and crossed the room. She tapped Mazie on the knee. "I need coffee," she whispered. "You want to come with me?"

Mazie nodded, welcoming the rescue from her own rapidly eroding good sense. Slipping out from underneath J.B.'s heavy arm, she grabbed her phone and wallet and followed his sister out of the waiting room. The sandwich shop and the main dining room were closed, but near the front entrance, a sleepy barista dozed over her iPad at a coffee counter.

Leila ordered her drink tall and black. Mazie couldn't face that much caffeine in the middle of the night, but she asked for an iced green tea. They found seats in the nearby atrium.

Mazie smiled sympathetically at the other woman. "This must have been really scary for all of you."

"Terrifying." Leila buried her nose in her cup. "My mom is a superhero. Seeing her like this…" She sniffed and wiped her nose.

"Were there any symptoms?"

"Honestly? I don't know. She's the kind of person who would badger the rest of us to get flu shots and go to the dentist, but she might have ignored her own warning signs 'cause she's always so busy."

"Heart surgeons perform miracles these days."

"Yeah." Leila yawned and set her empty cup on a nearby table. "I'm sorry our family drama ruined your special night."

"Oh, that's okay," Mazie said quickly, wincing inwardly. The ground beneath her feet was quicksand. How did a recently engaged woman react? "The important thing is for your mom to be okay."

Leila grinned, seemingly fortified by her java. "To be honest, I was pretty shocked about this engagement. After the debacle of J.B.'s first marriage, he swore he'd never tie the knot again." Her eyes rounded, and she slapped a hand over her mouth. "Oh, lordy. Please tell me you already knew about that…the marriage, I mean."

"Of course. He's been very upfront with me. You do remember that my brothers and I used to hang out at your house all the time? Not so much as adults, but enough to keep up with J.B. and his escapades. He told me his wife was pretty awful."

"Mom and Dad tried to stop him, but he was madly in love. I was just starting high school, so I thought it was all terribly romantic. It didn't take long for the truth to come out. All she wanted was money. Poor J.B. was collateral damage."

"He seems to have bounced back pretty well," Mazie said, hoping she didn't sound cynical.

"I haven't seen him go out with the same woman more than two or three times. He's rabid about not giving anyone of the opposite sex the wrong idea. He's a workaholic, and he's not interested in anything permanent." She frowned and cocked her head. "How did the two of you hook up? I've watched you avoid each other for years."

"Ah, well…" This was the tough part. She was a terrible liar. "We occasionally crossed paths at a party or a gallery opening. But I suppose we got closer when he started this renovation project down near the Battery. He wants to buy my property. I kept saying no, and he continued to beg."

"Interesting. I've known my brother to do just about anything to seal a deal, but marriage? That's a new one."

Mazie knew Leila was teasing. But her careless comments underscored Mazie's own insecurities. If Mazie had said yes when J.B.'s Realtor called the first time, or even the second, Mazie never would have gone out with J.B., and she never would have been put in the situation of lying to his family.

"Shouldn't we get back upstairs?" she said.

Leila nodded, all animation fading from her face. "Definitely."

As they walked into the surgical lounge, Alana updated her sister with the latest progress report. J.B. and his dad appeared to be asleep.

Mazie kept to herself in one corner of the room until she realized that a *real* fiancée would never be standoffish. Instead, she moved to sit close to J.B., hoping that his sisters would think she didn't want to wake him.

At four fifteen, a weary surgeon came in to talk to them. The siblings formed a united front around their father. The doctor was upbeat. "The surgery went as expected. We did a quadruple bypass, so she'll have a long road ahead of her. Healing takes months, not weeks."

J.B.'s expression was strained. "When can we see her?"

"She'll be in recovery for some time. We'll rouse her slowly. When she's awake, we want everything to be low-key and calm. Nothing stressful at all. I'd recommend all of you go home and get a few hours of sleep. Come back later in the morning. If there's any problem, a nurse will contact you immediately."

Mr. Vaughan didn't like that answer. Mazie could tell. But the poor man looked dead on his feet.

Leila put an arm around her dad. "Alana and I will go back to the house with you, Papa."

J.B. kissed the top of her head. "Thanks, sis." He hugged his father and Alana. "I'll take Mazie home and then see you guys around lunchtime."

Leila frowned. "But you live the closest of any of us to the hospital."

J.B. didn't miss a beat. "Mazie doesn't," he said.

Mazie could see the speculation in their gazes, but she was too tired to play her part. Did the girls think J.B. would have a fiancée living under his roof already? Fat chance. She'd had it from his own sister's lips that the man didn't like relationships.

In the parking lot, she tried to lobby for common sense. "Let me call a car," she said. "There's no reason at all for you to drive me home."

They had come straight from their date to the hospital. Her car was out at the beach house.

J.B. destroyed her argument by kissing her deep and

slow. His tongue stroked hers. "There's a better option," he muttered, as he turned her legs to spaghetti. "For once, just trust me."

Ten

"Trust you?" Mazie eyed him warily.

He grimaced. "I'm so tired my eyeballs ache. Leila was right. It will be dawn soon. I don't really want to spend the next hour driving you to the beach and then heading back to my own place. Come home with me," he said huskily. "My house is five minutes away. We both need sleep."

Mazie hesitated. This family crisis had thrust her into a position of intimacy that was difficult to handle. She was a compassionate person. She could see that J.B. was dealing with stress and fatigue. Still, her sense of self-preservation was strong.

She'd been avoiding this connection forever, and now here it was, rushing her far too quickly into the quicksand of shared desire and impulsive choices.

"I'll be fine in a cab."

He took her wrist and reeled her in, wrapping his arms around her and pulling her close. "Pretty please, Mazie Jane. I don't want to be alone."

She examined his face in the harsh glow of the security lights. If she had seen even a shred of evidence that he was playing her, she would have walked away. But the hell of it was, she thought he was sincere.

"Okay," she said, giving in more or less gracefully. "It will only be for a few hours anyway."

They both climbed into the vehicle without further conversation. J.B. drove with a steady hand on the wheel. His profile was stark. Bold forehead, straight nose, firm chin. Mazie felt as if she was seeing him for the first time. It was clear that his family adored him and that he was someone they leaned on.

At his house, she hovered in the hallway. "I'll crash down here," she said. "Why don't you go on upstairs and get comfortable?"

He frowned. "I have a perfectly lovely guest room right across the hall from my suite."

"I don't want to argue about this J.B. Not right now." If she climbed those stairs, all bets were off. Too cozy. Too everything.

His gaze cooled. "Fine. We'll share the sofa."

She'd had no sleep. Her eyes were gritty, and her body was limp with exhaustion. "If that's what you want."

Most of J.B.'s beautiful home was decorated in true Charleston fashion. No doubt one or both of his sisters had helped, maybe even Jane. But at the back of the house in his personal den, he had opted for masculine comfort. An enormous flat-screen TV. A couple of huge recliners and an oversize sofa that looked as if it was covered in the soft, scarred leather of old aviator jackets.

He kicked off his shoes and grabbed two afghans from the cabinet to the left of the TV. "Make yourself at home. Are you hungry? Thirsty?"

She shook her head, wondering why she had voluntarily stepped into the lion's den. "I'm fine. Go to sleep, J.B. You'll have to be back at the hospital soon." Without waiting to see if he would take her advice, she curled up on one end of the couch and laid her head on the arm. At the last minute, she remembered to send a text to Gina letting her know that Mazie would not be coming in to the store this morning...or at least not until much later. Then she silenced her phone.

Out of the corner of her eye, she saw J.B. sprawl a few feet away from her and prop his feet on the coffee table.

The lure of sleep was strong. How did she end up here? Was this really as innocent as it seemed?

J.B. groaned and rolled his neck. "I'm too damn tired to relax."

Mazie sighed. "Lie down, for heaven's sake. Let me rub your head."

"I can think of other places I'd rather have you rub." His fake leer didn't have enough energy to be insulting.

"On your back, Mr. Vaughan."

As she sat up, J.B. stretched out full-length, his feet propped on the other arm of the sofa. With his head in her lap, he relaxed. Thick lashes, unfairly beautiful for a man, settled on his cheeks.

"Thank you, Mazie," he muttered.

She stroked his forehead, feeling the silkiness of his hair. Keeping her touch light and steady, she watched as the lines of tension in his face and shoulders gradually eased.

Some strong emotion slid through her veins and weakened her resolve. She couldn't fool herself any longer. She was dangerously close to falling for him again. How reckless could she be?

Soon, he was asleep. Only then did she allow herself to lean back and close her eyes.

J.B. dreamed about angels. Perhaps he should have been alarmed. He wasn't prepared for his life to end. But this particular angel whispered to him, words he couldn't quite catch.

He awoke with a start. For several long seconds confusion reigned. Then the familiar surroundings grounded him. Worry for his mother arrived first. And then concern about Mazie.

Good Lord. How long had he been sleeping in her lap? The poor woman must be a glutton for punishment. He sat up carefully, noting the awkward bend to her neck. A glance at his watch told him it was not quite eight thirty. Still time to rest. And no messages on his phone.

Without overthinking it, he grabbed a pillow and scooped Mazie up long enough to change their positions. She murmured in her sleep but didn't wake. With his back against the couch, he tucked her up against him and sighed. This would do.

The scent of her hair tickled his nose. He had danced around his attraction to her for years, never quite willing to admit it existed. Now here she was. In his house. In his arms.

This relationship was *snakebit* from the begin-

ning. Even if Mazie learned to trust him, what did he
need from her? Marriage was out of the question. He'd
learned that lesson the hard way.

Women were duplicitous. And he was bad at reading their wants and intentions.

He closed his eyes for the second time, and slept.

When next he awoke, the sun poured into the room
through a crack in the draperies. As he crooked his
arm to see his watch, Mazie stirred. "J.B.?"

"Right here, darlin'. We both went out cold."

She appeared charmingly befuddled. "Oh."

He stroked her cheek with the pad of his thumb.
"Are you always this beautiful in the morning?"

It was a cheesy line. But hell, it was true. Her skin
was soft and flushed. Those big golden eyes were underscored with shadows, but still deep enough for a
man to lose himself.

Mazie bit her lip. "I must look a mess."

He threaded his fingers through her thick, glorious
hair. The waves clung to his hand. His heart beat faster.
"I'm going to kiss you."

It was a warning and a plea all wrapped up in one.
He felt remarkably off his game. Ever since that incredible episode in the bank vault, he'd been obsessed
with the need to touch her again.

He'd been compelled to ask her out. Some would
say it was his subconscious that had taken over and
proclaimed the false engagement.

He shifted his weight and leaned over her on one
elbow. "Mazie," he whispered.

She put a hand behind his head and pulled him
closer. "Yes."

The single word shot arousal through his veins like

a powerful stimulant. He was trembling, almost out of control. Yet they had barely begun.

Her lips clung to his, not submissive, but challenging. He was hard in an instant. Desperate. Ready to beg. But the incredible woman beneath him was not erecting any barriers at all. She arched into his embrace, melding their bodies from shoulders to hips, completely his except for the fact that they were fully clothed.

The look in her eyes was his undoing, part yearning, part caution. She didn't completely trust him. He'd have to work on that.

"Easy, love." He distracted her with a hungry kiss while he wrestled with her thin sweater. Once he ripped the garment over her head, he was treated to the sight of raspberry-tipped breasts cupped in a lacy confection that was meant to drive a man wild.

He teased her nipples through the semi-transparent cloth. "I've pictured you like this in my head," he groaned. "But I never thought it would happen."

She nipped his bottom lip with sharp teeth. "And why is that? I thought the larger-than-life J.B. Vaughan was irresistible to the female sex."

"You're sassy. And no, I'm not irresistible. You aren't even sure you like me, Mazie Jane. And you sure as hell don't trust me."

The flicker of her gold-tipped eyelashes told him he had hit a nerve. But her voice when she answered was steady. "I discovered something in that bank vault, J.B. Something that shocked me. Apparently, it's possible to crave someone even if he's a bad boy with a terrible reputation."

His smile widened. "You *crave* me, darlin'? Well, I must be doing *something* right."

"Does your ego ever take a rest?" She caressed his chin, smiling faintly.

He ignored her gibe. "Get undressed before someone like your brother decides to interrupt us."

Mazie wriggled away from him long enough to dispense with her pants and socks. J.B. did the same. He leaned forward to grab his wallet and extract a condom. His hands were shaking.

She curled her arms around him from behind and rested her cheek on his back. "We're probably going to regret this."

"Yeah. Maybe." He pulled her in front of him, standing her on her feet and kissing her cute, tiny belly button. Gooseflesh rose on her pale skin. "You have no idea how much I want you."

"That might be the sleep deprivation talking."

He slid her bikini underwear down her legs and sighed. "Nope. It's you, Mazie Jane." He parted her damp folds with his thumbs and caressed her intimately. Her whimper of pleasure hardened his erection a millimeter more, if that was possible.

In another situation, he would have taken his time with her. He might have paused to savor the smorgasbord of delights. But he'd only been half kidding about Jonathan. Given the situation at the hospital, someone could call at any moment. He dared not turn off his phone.

"We should hurry," she panted, perhaps reading his mind. "I'm ready for you. More than ready." She played with the shell of his ear, leaning down to whisper naughty suggestions.

J.B. cursed. He shed his boxers with more speed than finesse and sheathed his sex. Mazie was still wearing her bra. It was too late to do anything about it. He had to have her in the next thirty seconds, or he was going to die.

Moving to the edge of the sofa, he gripped her wrist. "Come here, sweet thing. Let me love you." He took her by the waist and helped her straddle his lap, her long, smooth legs spread on either side of his hips.

Mazie took over before he could do more than groan and bury his face in her chest. She sank down onto him, taking him inside her, joining their bodies with the sweet wild slide of passion.

His vision went dark. Everything inside him focused on the sensation of Mazie's tight, hot sex accepting him. Sweat broke out on his brow. "Slower," he begged. He was close to embarrassing both of them.

Mazie combed his hair with both hands, massaging his scalp, toying with his ears. "What if I like it fast and hard?"

He gripped her soft butt so tightly it might leave bruises. "Bad girl." He thrust upward, filling her, claiming her.

Mazie laughed. The soft, husky chuckle drove him mad. Suddenly, he was sorry he had chosen this position. It was too passive. He was in a volatile mood. Lack of sleep blurred the edges of his control.

"Put your legs around my waist." He stood abruptly. Mazie was a tall woman, but he was extremely motivated. He eased past the coffee table and tumbled them both to the carpet, their bodies still joined.

Mazie smiled up at him, her eyelids half closed, her

breath coming in short pants. "Who knew you were so strong? I'm impressed Mr. Vaughan."

His chest heaved. "You make me nuts. Why is that, do you think?"

"Mutual antipathy?"

He pumped his hips.

Her eyelids fluttered shut. She arched her back, gasping.

"Look at me, Mazie. I want to see your eyes when you come."

She obeyed. Her amber-gold gaze locked on to his. He felt naked suddenly, raw and exposed. Those eyes saw everything.

Mazie wet her lips with the tip of her tongue. She reached up and traced his features with her thumbs. "I won't break, J.B. Give it all to me."

The sexual challenge dissolved the last of his rapidly winnowing willpower. With a groan of helpless inevitability, he pounded into her, thrusting again and again until his world went black, and his entire body spasmed in hot, desperate pleasure.

Dimly, he heard Mazie's cry of release and felt the flutters of her sex on his shaft as she came.

When it was over, they lay in a tangle of arms and legs and fractured breathing. Mazie was still wearing her bra. J.B. couldn't feel his legs. Her body was soft and warm beneath his. He never wanted to move, though that wasn't a viable choice under the circumstances.

After several long moments of silence, he rolled to his back and cleared his throat. "I don't know what to say. I'd offer to fix you bacon and eggs, but that seems a paltry thank-you for what just happened."

He was dizzy, and his feet were cold.

Mazie patted his cheek. "Don't be silly. It was sex. Great sex, I'll admit. But just sex. I can grab breakfast at home."

When she stood up, found her undies and began to get dressed, he gaped at her. "What are you doing?"

She pointed at the antique clock on the mantel. "It's late, J.B. Your family will be expecting you at the hospital. And even though I told Gina that I wouldn't be there to open the shop, I still need to get to work." She fastened her jeans and sat down to put on her socks and shoes.

"But you're the boss." What the hell was happening? The sex had been incredible, wild and hot. How could she pretend as if nothing had happened? Was she really as unaffected as she seemed?

"It's the Christmas shopping season. I need to be at my store. But more important, your mother will be asking for you soon. Grab your shower, J.B. I'll call a car service. No worries."

She picked up her purse and jacket. "I'll be in touch to check on your mom later today." She blew him a kiss. "Gotta run."

As he rolled to his knees and stood up, he heard his front door open and shut.

Eleven

Mazie leaned her back against J.B.'s front door for half a second, barely long enough to catch her breath, and then she fled. She jogged three blocks before she called a car service, desperate to make sure J.B. wasn't going to follow her. With her heart pounding and her eyes blinking back tears, she felt like a crazy woman.

Her whole world was upended.

How could puppy love have stayed alive all these years? She *knew* what kind of man J.B. was. Thanks to his sister's candid remarks, Mazie also knew J.B.'s views on relationships and marriage.

Only the worst kind of masochist would allow herself to be sucked back into his realm. Pretending like morning sex was no big deal had required all of her acting abilities. Harder still was erasing the mental image of a naked J.B. sprawled on the plush carpet.

The man had a seriously ripped body.

He was also funny and smart, and kind to his mother and the rest of his family. That didn't erase his willingness to squash other people in his drive to get what he wanted in business.

He had hurt her once before. If she allowed him to get too close, odds were, it would happen again.

Despite her panic and all-out flight from J.B., she arrived home in a slightly calmer frame of mind. She would survive whatever this was. She had to…the past was not worth repeating.

Jonathan was at work, of course. She had texted him from the car to let him know Mrs. Vaughan was stable. He had answered with a single word. *Good.* That kind of clipped response was typical of her brother when he was neck deep in shipping crises.

Her father was dozing in the living room with a paperback novel in his lap. Mazie sat down beside him and touched his arm. "Hi, Daddy."

He opened his eyes. "Hello, baby. What are you doing home this time of day?"

She explained about Mrs. Vaughan's heart attack, glossing over the details about her date with J.B. and why Mazie was at the hospital at all.

Her father nodded. "I'll have Jonathan's assistant send flowers."

"That would be lovely." She paused, shifting gears. "How was *your* dinner last night? Did you have a good time?"

He grew animated as he shared details of his evening.

Mazie spotted an opportunity and took it. "Daddy, have you ever thought about moving to one of those places where your friends live? Here at the house you're awfully isolated and lonely, and besides, you know that Jonathan and I might not always be around."

"I like it here," he said. "It's safe." Then his smile grew wistful. "Are you planning on leaving your old dad, Mazie? I knew it would happen one day."

"No plans," she said lightly, witnessing his frail emotions. This thing with J.B. had made her even more aware of how dysfunctional her family was. She sighed, needing reassurance, wanting answers. "Daddy, please tell me what happened with Hartley. Jonathan won't talk about it."

His face darkened. "And neither will I. It's best you don't know. Just understand that he's probably never coming back."

She wasn't a child. What secret was so terrible that it had ripped their small family apart?

With an inward sigh, she stood and stretched, feeling the strain of not enough sleep and the fact that several of those hours she did doze were sitting upright on J.B.'s sofa. It was frightening to realize that she already missed him. "I'm going to take a shower, grab a quick lunch and head to work. Do you need anything before I go?"

His eyelids were already drooping. "I'm right as rain. Don't worry about me."

Fortunately for Mazie, All That Glitters was madly busy on this bright, sunny Saturday in December.

She waded into the fray, grateful for something to distract her from the unanswerable questions about her fake engagement and her enigmatic fiancé.

Since Gina was far too busy to dig for details about

Mazie's date and the events that followed, Mazie was able to shut out the past twenty-four hours. Mostly.

The day passed quickly. Sales numbers were gratifying. If she took the new building J.B. was offering her, she would have ample room to expand.

The Tarleton shipping business would have had room for her if she had been interested. But she had needed something she could control, a part of her life where she was in charge, where she didn't have to worry about being abandoned.

If she couldn't have J.B.—and did she really want him?—her work was going to be her future.

As they prepared to lock up and head home at five, Mazie cornered Gina. "You want to grab a bite of dinner?"

"Oh, gosh, Mazie. You know I would. But we're having a big extended-family Christmas thing at my aunt's house tonight. Kind of a command performance. You're welcome to come with me."

"No, no. That's fine. Go. Don't be late. I'll wrap things up."

"Are you sure?"

"Positive. You covered for me this morning. Get out of here."

When the store was empty, Mazie turned the deadbolt and flipped the sign in the window to Closed.

She told herself she wasn't jealous of Gina, but it was a lie. Gina came from a huge Italian clan. She had more cousins than she could count. Mazie's parents were both only children.

All Mazie had ever wanted was to belong, to have a big, loving family. First her mother was sent away. Then Hartley left. Now her father's health was precarious. Soon it would be just Jonathan and Mazie. When Jonathan eventually married, Mazie would be on her own.

The prospect was dismal. Was that why she had let herself be drawn back into J.B.'s orbit? Was it the memory of her old crush on him that drove her now, or was there more to this dangerous liaison?

It must be the holidays making her maudlin. As much as she loved the holly and the mistletoe and the beauty of the season, at times all the hoopla amplified her aloneness. She finished the last of the chores that were rote to her by now, and went to the back to get her jacket and purse.

When she returned, her heart stopped. There, standing half-visible in front of the top glass pane of her door, was a huge man. But a familiar one. He was dressed casually in khakis and a forest green sweater.

After her heart started beating again, she opened the lock and let him in. "You scared me to death," she said. It was already dark outside.

"It's dangerous for you to be closing up alone. Anyone could bust in here and hurt you or rob you."

"We have a system," she said calmly, though her fingernails dug into her palms. "Gina and I usually walk out together, but she had a *thing* tonight. I sent her on, so she wouldn't be late. What are you doing here, J.B.?"

He lifted an eyebrow. "Collecting my fiancée?"

"That's not funny." Even so, his teasing smile made her heart wobble. The fact that they had been naked together only a few hours before made her skittish.

"Mom's asking for you," he said.

"Well, crud." She frowned. "I know why you did

what you did, but how are we supposed to handle this now?"

"We need to buy a ring. I asked my friend Jean Philippe to give us a private appointment at six."

Mazie heart clenched in alarm. "We're not engaged," she said firmly. "And I'm not picking out a ring."

"You have to."

"I don't have to do anything."

"Be reasonable, Mazie. She's awake and she wants to see you. She's worried that her heart attack messed up our special evening. She's ragging my butt to make sure I put a ring on your finger. Sooner, not later. I couldn't disappoint her."

Mazie was appalled at how much she wanted to play his game. At this rate she would end up abandoned at the altar because she didn't have enough sense to guard her heart. "Tell her I'm picky. Tell her no one in Charleston has a loose stone big enough or perfect enough to suit me. Tell her you and I will be flying to New York after the holidays to hit up Harry Winston and Tiffany's."

"I can't tell her that," he said, visibly grinding his jaw.

"Why not?"

"Because she would insist I book two tickets right now. The woman is like a bulldog, Mazie. Sick or not sick, she'll grill you until you cave."

"Why don't you borrow a ring from a friend, then. Or pick out something by yourself. It can be anything. Why does it matter?"

J.B. didn't like not getting his own way. His eyes glittered. "I've never had to work so hard to buy a woman jewelry."

Mazie didn't want to think about all those women. "Sorry to inconvenience you," she muttered.

"My mom has spies all over the city. If I don't do this the right way, somebody will spill the truth and she'll be devastated."

"And you'll say it's my fault." She stared at him, shocked.

"Maybe."

Mazie saw a million reasons why this was a terrible idea. "She came through the surgery really well. Why don't you just admit the truth?"

"You mean I should say that I flat-out lied to her on her death bed? Oh, yeah. That's an awesome idea."

"Well, when you put it like that..." Mazie grimaced. That was the trouble with lies. One thing always led to another. "This is ridiculous, J.B. I *know* Jean Philippe. Not as well as you, maybe, but I'm pretty sure he's not going to buy my act as an adoring fiancée."

"I thought about that. We'll just tell him that we've kept our relationship under wraps."

"Why?"

"I don't know. Maybe your brother doesn't approve."

"Oh, crap." She rubbed the center of her forehead where a headache bloomed. "I'm going to have to tell Jonathan and Daddy what we're doing. If word gets back to them that I'm *engaged*, and I haven't told them, they'll be so hurt."

"Can your father keep a secret?"

"Are you asking me if he's senile?"

"Well, he does seem to be slipping."

Mazie shook her head slowly. "He's not as sharp as he was, but he'll understand this. I'll just have to re-mind him not to talk about it at all. That's the safest bet. Besides, it's only for a week or so…right? Until your mom is recovering well? Then you and I can have a huge fight and end things."

"You don't have to sound so happy about it," J.B. groused.

She moved toward the door and stopped to pat his cheek. "It's going to be the highlight of my Christmas season."

If there was one thing Mazie knew about J.B., it was that he never left any detail to chance. That's why he was such a success in business. That and the fact that he was way smarter than his smiling blue eyes and surfer physique might suggest.

She stood on the sidewalk outside her shop and argued with him. "I'm taking my own car," she said. "It's the only plan that makes sense. That way I can drop by the hospital after we do this jewelry thing, and then head home."

"A couple buying an engagement ring doesn't arrive in multiple vehicles," he said stubbornly. "You have to commit to the role, Mazie."

"We'll improvise. It will be okay." She wasn't going to let him push her around. It was a matter of principle.

"Fine."

J.B. wasn't happy, but she didn't care. She was tired, and this pretending was breaking her heart. Didn't she deserve a man who *really* wanted her?

As far as she could tell, J.B. was simply being himself…taking care of problems. His determination to bend her will to his shouldn't have hurt. She knew who and what he was. But her emotions plummeted.

Jean Philippe's shop made All That Glitters look

like a thrift store. He was a fixture in Charleston. He sold wedding rings and engagement rings, fabulous necklaces and even the occasional tiara. The fifty-something jeweler knew all there was to know about gem stones and their provenance.

Clearly, he didn't offer private appointments to anyone and everyone. He was expecting a big sale.

The store was closed, of course, since it was after business hours. A uniformed guard, fully armed, unlocked the front door and let them in. Then he relocked the plate-glass entrance and stationed himself beside the exit.

Jean Philippe was effusive. "Mr. Vaughan, Ms. Tarleton. I am honored that I can serve you in this special way."

Mazie's cheeks heated. "We'll try to be fast. I wasn't sure I wanted a ring, but J.B. insisted."

The older man raised a scandalized eyebrow. "Of *course* you need a ring. Oh, I know how you girls think these days. You're independent. You can buy your own jewelry. You don't need a man. But trust me, young lady, it means far more coming from the love of your life."

When Mazie glanced at J.B., he had an odd look on his face. Maybe he was jittery about the *L* word. "So how do we start?" she asked.

Jean Philippe glanced at J.B. "Would you like to select a handful of rings and let your fiancée pick from those, or do I—"

J.B. shook his head ruefully. "I'll let her have free rein. I trust her."

The other man's carefully manicured eyebrows shot

to his hairline. There were pieces in this store that would bankrupt a lot of men. "Well, I…"

"Anything she wants, Jean. Anything."

It was all Mazie could do not to roll her eyes. Her *fiancé* was having entirely too much fun at her expense. It would serve him right if she picked out the biggest, gaudiest bauble in the store.

Unfortunately, she was too squeamish to spend that kind of money for a two-week stint of playacting.

Without much fanfare, she glanced in the nearest case. "That one's nice," she said.

Jean Philippe pulled out the ring she had indicated, a tiny frown marring his forehead. "A decent stone," he said grudgingly. "But rather pedestrian. It's only a single carat."

Mazie jumped, startled, when J.B. slid an arm around her waist. He murmured in her ear. "I'm a wealthy man, darlin'. We need something that befits my bride-to-be. Something that's as beautiful as you are. Don't hold back."

The jeweler nodded eagerly. "Indeed."

Oh, good grief.

She stared at the rows of rings blindly, wishing J.B. didn't smell so good. Also wishing that he would back up so she could breathe.

One at a time, she pointed out rings. One at a time, the two men shot them down. Finally, she began to lose patience.

She took J.B.'s arm. "Perhaps we should come back another day when we have more time. I want to visit your mother."

J.B. ignored her, his attention riveted on a nearby case she hadn't perused.

"That one," he said. "Top row on the right."

Jean Philippe practically danced in his polished cordovans. "Wonderful eye you have, Mr. Vaughan. That is an exquisite yellow diamond from Brazil. The rich color and dazzling clarity are unmatched by anything I've seen in the last ten years. Five and a half carats, cushion cut. The setting is platinum, very simple. Designed to showcase the stone, but if the lady prefers something else, we could always reset."

J.B. narrowed his eyes and picked up the loupe. "Let me take a look."

As he examined the stone, Mazie freaked inwardly. The ring had to be well over six figures. That was a heck of a lot of money for a play prop.

She tugged his sleeve. "That one's too much. Be sensible."

J.B. turned to face her, his half smile intimate, toe-curling. "It's you, Mazie. Rare. Unique. Stunning. The stone picks up the sunshine color in your amber eyes and the gleams of gold in your hair." Before she could stop him, he took her left hand and slid the ring onto her third finger.

For a split second, the world stopped. J.B.'s hands holding hers were warm, his grasp strong. The ring nestled in place as if it had been sized for her and her alone.

She swallowed. "It's beautiful." The stone was actually heavy on her hand. Weighty. Serious.

Everything this engagement was not.

He frowned, perhaps sensing her unease. "We can go with a traditional diamond if you'd prefer. I realize this color is not the usual bridal choice."

Mazie knew J.B. was playing a part. He was pretending to care, pretending to consult her wishes. No matter how much she told herself this fairy-tale moment wasn't real, the little girl inside her who dreamed of fairy tales and Prince Charming was jumping up and down.

Her throat was tight. "I love it," she said huskily.

J.B. turned to the jeweler, pulling his wallet from his jacket pocket and extracting his platinum credit card. "We'll take it."

Twelve

Mazie found a parking spot at the hospital, turned off the engine and sat for a moment, staring at her newly adorned hand. If alien civilizations actually existed, she could probably pick up communications from other planets on this thing. The ring was huge, stunning.

Even here, in the semidarkness, it seemed to have a life of its own, much like J.B.'s impromptu engagement for his mother's benefit.

Before Mazie and J.B. had left the jewelry store, Mazie had been forced to hover for long embarrassing minutes while the two men conducted the business portion of the transaction. The ring came with a two-page appraisal and a fancy box wrapped in plum satin paper and silver ribbon.

The fact that the box was empty didn't seem to bother anyone. It was part of the pomp and circumstance of purchasing a ridiculously expensive piece of jewelry.

She glanced out the window, suddenly aware—as never before—of the possibility of getting mugged in a parking lot. Because she had insisted on having her own car, she and J.B. had gotten separated on the way to the hospital. He might be close by or on the other side of the building.

As far as she could tell, no was one lurking in the shadows ready to snatch a ring off her finger. Shaking her head at her own vivid imagination, she got out and locked her car.

Before she could take more than a few steps, J.B. appeared, loping across the pavement. Clearly, he had found a parking spot more quickly than she had.

"Did you spend most of the day here?" she asked.

He folded his arms across his chest. "The part of it that I wasn't having sex with you, Mazie. You can't pretend it didn't happen."

"Watch me," she muttered, taking off for the hospital entrance as if she were being pursued.

J.B. kept pace with her mad dash, but he didn't touch her. She told herself she was glad.

In the elevator, they were surrounded by strangers. On the CCU floor, the other three Vaughans kept their vigil. J.B.'s mother was doing very well. The nurses had had her up walking, and all her stats were good. In another twenty-four to forty-eight hours, she would likely be moved to a regular room.

Alana motioned for everyone's attention. "Mama wants to tell us something. But we have to make it quick. They're bending the rules right and left, but we're running out of goodwill, I think."

The five of them entered the cubicle. The two sisters took one side of the bed, J.B. and his father the other. Mazie hung back near the door.

"Okay, Mama," Alana said. "What's up?"

Mrs. Vaughan looked at her son. "You four have been here most of the day." She patted her son's hand. "J.B., I want you to take your sisters and your dad, and go have a nice restaurant dinner somewhere. *Not* the hospital cafeteria. Mazie will sit with me while you're gone."

They all turned and looked at Mazie. She felt her face heat. "I'd be happy to do that."

Leila grimaced. "But Mazie needs dinner."

"I have peanut butter crackers in my purse. I'll be fine." She curled her fingers around the ring. Maybe she could slip it off for the moment.

J.B.'s face had no expression at all. If Mazie had to guess, she'd say he was sifting through his mother's statement for hidden grenades and wondering if it was safe to leave Mazie behind.

Mrs. Vaughan waved a hand. "Go. I'm serious." Her voice was weak, but her color was healthy, and she was clearly in good spirits.

"Okay, Mama." J.B. turned to Mazie and kissed her on the cheek. "Make my mother behave."

"I'll do my best." Having J.B. be so casually affectionate after what had happened between them this morning rattled her composure. What would happen if his careful attentions were rooted in truth? Could she trust him? Would she be glad?

When the room emptied, Jane Vaughan exhaled and smiled at Mazie. "I love that crew, but when they hover, I want to smack them up the side of the head.

I'm not accustomed to being out of control. I don't much care for it."

"Yes, ma'am. I understand."

"Pull that chair closer to the bed, Mazie."

"You probably should rest until they bring your dinner tray. I have things to read on my iPad."

J.B.'s mother shook her head. "This may be our only chance to speak in private. I have to carpe diem," she said.

Seize the day? Mazie frowned inwardly. "I'm not sure I understand."

"I want to talk about my son, dear girl. And your relationship to him."

Mazie froze, sensing danger. Here was a woman who had undergone serious surgery. She couldn't be upset or shocked or any other emotion that would impede her recovery. "Okay..."

Jane chuckled. "Don't look so petrified. I know the engagement is fake. You can relax."

Mazie gaped at her. "Why would you say that?"

"Jackson Beauregard is my firstborn. I know him, and I love him. Ever since that stupid woman coaxed him into marriage and humiliated him, J.B. has closed himself off emotionally. I've prayed that he would come to terms with the mistake he made, but J.B. is harder on himself than anyone else. He can't forgive his own youthful blunder. He swore never to let any other woman get that close to him again. And he's kept that vow. He has multiple women in his life, but to him they're as interchangeable as a pair of socks."

"But..."

The older woman grimaced. "He was trying to give me a reason to live. And it was sweet of him, dear boy.

But I'm not a fool. Nobody does a one-eighty that fast. If he had been falling in love with you, I would have gotten wind of it." She grinned. "I have *spies* all over the city."

"That's what J.B. told me." Mazie paused, trying to understand. "So you're saying there's no reason to continue with the charade?"

"Oh, no, my dear. Just the opposite. I'm begging you to keep up the pretense in hopes that my sweet boy will see that true love is worth fighting for."

Mazie's head was spinning. In the midst of this extraordinary conversation, a nurse had come in to draw blood and check vitals. Close on her heels was an employee with a dinner tray.

When the medical staff finally wrapped up their assigned tasks and left the room, Mazie uncovered the meal. "Looks like a grilled chicken breast, rice and lemon Jell-O."

"Oh, goody."

Jane's dour sarcasm made Mazie laugh. "You need the calories to get better. Which do you want first?"

"If I eat all that dreadful stuff, you have to agree to my plan."

Mazie cut up the chicken, added sweetener and lemon to the tea at Jane's request, and raised the head of the bed. "I'm feeling a little bit under the gun, Jane. You have to understand, J.B. and I are…" She trailed off.

How exactly did one define what she and J.B. were to each other? She was letting his masculine charm drag her under his spell all over again, and he was using her as a convenient ploy.

Jane, true to her word, was working her way through the bland food. "Have you slept together?"

"Ah…" A hot flush rose from Mazie throat to her hairline. This woman had endured major, life-threatening surgery, and yet still had the capacity to do an interrogation that would make a seasoned professional proud. "I'm not comfortable discussing that with you."

"Fair enough." Jane finished the rice. "I'm aware you've known each other forever, but how did you come to be on a fancy date last night?"

Mazie chose and discarded explanations rapidly. "J.B. was wining and dining me because he wants to buy my building. It's smack in the middle of his big restoration project. I'm the last holdout."

"How delicious. I hope you haven't made it easy for him."

Were they talking about business or sex?

Mazie uncovered the tiny serving of Jell-O and added a plastic spoon. "I'll have to admit, it made me mad that he thought I would simply give him what he wanted. So I've been cranky and obstructive. But he's offered me another property for my store that is lovely. I've decided to let him stew until after Christmas, and then give him what he needs."

"Well, I'm glad his business dealings are doing well, but I'm more concerned about his emotional wellbeing. Please let the engagement stand, Mazie. He already trusts you. That's a huge step forward."

"Why would you say that?" She couldn't let herself believe the fantasy that J.B. actually cared for her. There would be too far to fall when the truth was revealed.

"No man enters into a fake engagement unless he is

absolutely sure the woman in question will let him off
the hook when the charade is over. Clearly, he trusts
you not to sue him for breach of promise or something awful like that. And he doesn't have to worry
that you're after his money, because you have plenty
of your own. You're the perfect woman for him."

But she wasn't.

J.B. didn't want to be married. And no matter how
great the sex, no man was going to tie the knot when he
wasn't emotionally involved. Mazie wasn't convinced
J.B. would allow himself to be that vulnerable.

If she went along with this plan, he might destroy
her all over again. Still, she couldn't say no to his
mother, not under these circumstances.

"I don't know that I am, Jane. But if it will make you
happy, I'll let this arrangement ride for the moment."

Jane beamed. "Thank you dear. Now let me see
the ring."

Mazie blushed again. "How did you know?"

"You've been hiding your left hand since you walked
into the room. Not only that, I practically ordered my
son to take you ring shopping today, and I was fairly
certain he wanted to pacify me."

"It's a little over the top," Mazie confessed.

She held out her left hand. Even now, in this sterile,
medical setting, the ring blazed with life.

Jane took Mazie's hand in both of hers and studied
the diamond from all angles. "Wow," she said.

Mazie wrinkled her nose. "I know. It's too much,
isn't it? I don't know what he was thinking."

"I always told my children to go big or go home."
Jane closed her eyes, rubbing her chest absently.

"Mrs. Vaughan? Jane?" Mazie looked at her in alarm. "Are you okay?"

"Just tired, my dear. Why don't you read your book now, and I'll nap for a few minutes…"

"Of course." Mazie tidied the mostly empty food tray and covered everything. Then she rolled the little table away from the bed so Jane could relax in comfort.

When she glanced at her watch, she saw that the Vaughans had been gone only fifty minutes. If they followed Jane's directive, they would stay away another hour. Mazie pulled her iPad mini from her purse and queued up the book she was reading. It was a romantic comedy about a dyslexic librarian and a handyman who liked to work after hours. The story was charming and funny, but it failed to hold her interest.

At last, she dropped the device into her purse and studied the woman in the bed. Mothers, in general, were supposed to have keen instincts when it came to the love lives of their children. Jane was more dialed in than most. The fact that she saw through the false engagement ruse meant that she really did understand how J.B.'s mind worked.

What the other woman *didn't* know was that J.B. had already rejected Mazie once. He had broken her heart. He'd left her vulnerable and hurting.

You could argue that something so long ago wasn't real or even very important. But Mazie still carried the scars. For J.B.'s mother, she would let this charade continue a few days or weeks.

Nothing more, though.

She was not going to be foolish enough to believe that the ring and the situation were anything more than a son's desire to cheer up his mom.

* * *

J.B. stood in the doorway of his mother's hospital room and studied the two women inside. His mother was napping. Every report they had received so far was promising. Surely that meant she was beyond the worst of the danger.

Beside the bed in an ugly recliner covered in faux leather, Mazie snoozed as well, one hand tucked beneath her cheek. It was no wonder. She had waited at the hospital with him a big chunk of the night, and then this morning at his house, she had been otherwise engaged.

The memory of making love to Mazie disturbed him. He liked keeping things in neat compartments. His feelings for the woman with the whiskey-colored hair and the amber eyes slopped over into several boxes.

Business contact. Longtime family friend. Childhood confidante. Lover.

Most disturbing of all, she was his best friend's sister. It was the last designation that gave him heartburn.

A physical relationship with Jonathan's sister seemed fraught with danger. For years he had kept her in a box labeled *not for* me. Now, to make things worse, J.B. himself had invented a fake engagement to give his mother something on which to focus her goals for recovery. How far would he have to play out that scenario before he put a stop to it?

Not that he thought Mazie would take advantage of the situation. If anything, she was a very reluctant fiancée.

He must have made a sound, because Mazie's eyes flew open.

"Oh, hey," she said. "You're back. Where are the others?"

His mom roused, as well. "Hello, son. Did you all get something good to eat?"

He nodded. "We did, Mom. Dad and the girls have gone home to sleep. I'm taking first shift. I'll be here overnight."

"I don't need a babysitter."

He leaned down and squeezed her hand. "Humor me." He glanced at Mazie. "If you're ready, I'll walk you down to your car."

"Take your time," his mother said with an arch smile.

Mazie's cheeks heated.

He rolled his eyes. "Behave, Mom."

She was unrepentant. "The moon is out. It's a beautiful night. I'm not going anywhere. And by the way..."

"Yes?"

"You did well on the ring. It's gorgeous."

For some reason, the tops of his ears got hot. "We're glad you like it. I wanted something unique and special... like Mazie."

His fiancée stood and stretched. The stone on her hand flashed and sparked as she moved. "Enough blarney," she said.

She gave his mom a smile. "I enjoyed talking to you, Jane. Maybe I'll see you tomorrow? If you feel like having a visitor?"

J.B.'s mother waved her arms. "Come here. Give me a hug. And yes, I'll be expecting you. I'll send the rest of them out for coffee, so we can gossip."

"As long as you're doing everything the doctor orders, we can gossip to your heart's content. Good night, Mrs. Vaughan. See you tomorrow."

"I'll be back shortly," J.B. said.

He took Mazie's arm and steered her toward the bank of elevators. "Thanks for doing that. It makes her feel good to know that the rest of us are obeying her orders."

"She's not that bad," Mazie protested. "She only wants what's best for all of you."

"Uh-oh," he said, faking alarm. "She's indoctrinated you."

Mazie punched his arm. "Don't be mean. Your mom is a sweetheart."

He tapped the button for the lobby. "I agree one hundred percent. But don't let her fool you. She'll have you dancing to her tune in no time."

Outside, he walked Mazie across the courtyard and to the far parking lot where she had left her car.

She unlocked the door and tossed her purse on the passenger seat. "You should hurry back inside," she said. "In case she needs something."

He leaned an arm on the roof of the car, boxing her in. "Trying to get rid of me, Ms. Tarleton?"

Mazie looked up at him, her features shadowed. "No."

He stroked a wisp of hair from her cheek, wishing they weren't in a public arena so he could kiss her the way he wanted, needed. "I missed you today."

She murmured something that was neither agreement nor dissent.

He frowned. "You *are* my fiancée, after all."

Her head snapped up, her demeanor indignant. "Fake fiancée," she insisted.

"What are we going to do about this *thing* between us?"

"You're talking about sex."

"Yes. But it's not easy and fun, is it? We're digging ourselves into a pretty big hole."

"I agree. It seems smarter to end things now."

"What if I don't want to? You and I are crazy in bed—crazy good."

"I'd like to point out that we haven't actually tried sex in a bed. We seem to go for more inappropriate locations. Bank vaults. Your living room sofa."

He kissed her temple. "Nothing wrong with a sofa." It struck him suddenly that he didn't want her to leave. He liked having her at arm's length in the midst of his family crisis. She made everything easier.

The implications of that shot alarm and adrenaline coursing through his veins, but he ignored the internal upheaval, intent on having his way.

"I have an idea," he said. "Why don't you move into my place for a few days? My mother likes you, and you could help us keep an eye on her. Plus, my house is close to All That Glitters. Cut your commute time in half."

"That's a fairly elaborate setup just so you and I can have the occasional booty call. What's your end game, J.B.?"

Why did women always want to strangle a man with emotion and romance? This was physical. Nothing more. Mazie had to know that.

"There is no end game," he said gruffly. "With Mom sick and you working and me *trying* to work, this is the only scenario I can come up with for you and I to get a moment alone."

"For sex."

"Yes," he said, grinding his jaw. "For sex."

"How long are you thinking about?"

"I don't know. A week, maybe. Or two."

"That takes us up until Christmas."

"I guess it does." He slid his hands into her hair and cupped her head, tilting it back so he could kiss her. "Spend Christmas with me, Mazie. Today wasn't enough," he said, his body already taut with need. "I want you. Beyond reason. Tell me you feel it, too."

She was soft and warm in his arms, her body a feminine foil for his harder, bigger frame.

"Yes," she said, her voice barely audible. She sounded more resigned than happy. "But I like a lot of things that are bad for me. Rich chocolate mousse. Salted caramel ice cream. Bad boys who insist on getting their own way."

He dragged her closer, closing the car door and leaning Mazie against it until his lower body pressed hers. His erection ached.

"I have to go back inside," he groaned.

Mazie cupped his face in her hands and kissed him slow and deep, her tongue teasing his. "I'll think about your offer, J.B." She flattened her palms on his chest and shoved. "We're not having sex in a parking lot. I have to draw the line somewhere."

He might have whimpered. He nearly begged. But she was right, damn it. Gulping in huge breaths of the chilled night air, he forced himself to back up. "Pack a bag tonight. Please."

"Don't push me. I said I'll think about it." Ducking out of his embrace, she opened the driver's door and got into her little sports car. "See you tomorrow."

Thirteen

Mazie was starving when she finally got home. She'd never actually gotten around to eating the peanut butter crackers in her purse. All of the household staff were long gone by now, but she could cook well enough on her own. Which was pretty surprising for a woman whose mother hadn't been around when she was a teenager. Fortunately, more than one housekeeper had taken pity on a moody preteen and let her putter around the kitchen.

Jonathan found her there. The smell of bacon frying had clearly drawn him away from his home office.

"Late dinner or early breakfast?" he asked, sniffing the air with an appreciative sigh.

She took a carton from the fridge. "I missed supper. You want any scrambled eggs?"

He sat on a stool at the counter. "Actually, that

sounds pretty damn good. I had a salad with a client, but I wasn't in the mood for a big meal."

"Still feeling rotten?"

He nodded. "I haven't wanted to tell you this, but I guess it's time. My doctor wants me to go to some hippie-dippie holistic retreat out in the desert to see if we can break the cycle of these headaches. The doctors and counselors who run the program use a combination of meditation and medical assessment and organic or natural medicines."

She tended the eggs carefully. The strips of perfectly crisped bacon were already draining on a paper towel.

"No offense, Jonathan, but that doesn't sound like you at all." His air of brooding exhaustion made her worry about him.

"You're right. In fact, you couldn't be *more* right. But I'm getting desperate."

"Here. I'll have toast ready in a minute. Start on this." She gave him the eggs and bacon. "But why wouldn't you want to tell me that?"

"Because the retreat center is booked months in advance. The only opening they had was the week that includes Christmas."

"Oh." Disappointment curled in her stomach. "Well, it's just one day on the calendar. Daddy and I will be fine."

Jonathan grimaced. "That's the other part. Dad's been invited to go on a cruise with his college buddies. He asked me what I thought, and I told him it would be good for him to get out of the house. But that was before I knew I'd be leaving, too. I feel terrible about this, Mazie. I've dreaded telling you."

She managed a smile. "Don't be ridiculous. I'm a

grown woman. Besides, there are tons of places I can celebrate the holiday. Don't worry about me at all. The important thing is for you to get well."

Relief lightened his face. "I'll make it up to you, I swear."

"I'll be fine. Eat your eggs before they get cold."

She added the toast to their plates and joined him. For several minutes, peace reigned in the beautiful kitchen. Mazie often thought about having her own place. A man to cook for, or one who might cook for her. A couple of kids running through the halls, leaving toys scattered about. Maybe a mongrel dog, or two...

"Jonathan?"

"Hmm?" He had cleared his plate and was now slathering butter and honey over a piece of toast.

"J.B.'s mother came through the surgery well. But right before she went under the knife, J.B. did something kind of dumb. They were all afraid she wasn't going to make it. Even Jane, his mom, wasn't sure."

"And?"

"J.B. told her we were secretly engaged. He said she had to get well so she could play with all the grandchildren we're going to have."

"Stupid bastard." But he said the words with wry affection.

"I know. I couldn't even be mad at him, because he was so worried and scared."

"But now you have to wait a little while before you can break it off so you won't upset her."

"Something like that." She didn't bother explaining that Jane Vaughan had already seen through the ruse. What did it matter?

Jonathan opened the dishwasher, tucking his few

items inside. "If you want my advice, I wouldn't bother telling Dad. It will only confuse him. I hate to say it, but I see him slipping a little more with each week that passes."

"And you think that won't be a problem on a cruise?"

Jonathan grinned. "It's not like he can wander off. Seriously, though, I know all of his gang. They'll look out for him."

"As long as none of them is like Daddy."

"The cruise is billed as an all-inclusive event for older adults. Much older. He'll be fine."

"I hope so."

Jonathan glanced at the clock. "Don't move. I have something I want to show you."

When he disappeared, Mazie tidied up the kitchen. The housekeeper could have done it in the morning, but Mazie hated leaving a mess overnight. She had just wiped down the counter when Jonathan returned carrying a small box, much the size of the one that had come with her ring.

This box was red leather, and it wasn't wrapped. Mazie was standing at the sink when Jonathan tucked his arms around her from behind. "I hate like hell to miss Christmas, sis. I want you to have your present early."

He hopped up on the granite-topped island and folded his arms across his chest. "Go ahead. Open it."

Mazie pulled on the hinged lid and caught her breath. Inside was a delicate necklace. A gold chain, featherlight, coiled in the box. It supported a single, gorgeous pearl, as fat as a child's marble.

She lifted the necklace carefully, rubbing a fingertip over the luminescent sphere. "It's beautiful, Jonathan."

"Dad put my name with his on a lot of legal stuff

recently. When I was going through the safety deposit box, I found a bunch of Mom's jewelry. Evidently, when he sent her away, she had to leave it all behind. I know how much you miss her, especially during the holidays. I thought you could wear this and feel close to her…until you and I can go to Vermont after the first of the year."

Mazie eyes were damp. "Thank you, Jonathan. I adore it."

He waited as she wrestled with the clasp. "It will all be yours someday anyway."

She frowned. "No. That's not fair. You and Hartley will take a share for your spouses."

"Hartley is out of the picture, and I don't know that marriage is in the cards for me."

"Why do you say that?"

His gaze was stormy, troubled. "I've wondered if these headaches are a precursor of something worse. What if I've inherited Mom's instability? I don't want to doom a wife or a baby to the kind of life you and I experienced. It wouldn't be fair."

She was shocked. Had he been wrestling with this possibility for months? Shaking her head vehemently, she touched his knee. "Oh, Jonathan. I had no idea. I don't think that could be true. You're brilliant. You run a multinational shipping empire. Hundreds of people depend on you, and you handle it all with such grace, including your ability to make sure Daddy still feels needed. You're *not* going crazy. I would tell you if I saw any inkling."

Some of the clouds left his face. "Thanks," he said gruffly.

"Don't worry about the holidays," she said. "I might

spend Christmas somewhere else since you and Daddy will both be gone." Was she rationalizing her decision? Trying to put a positive spin on a choice she knew she should never make? "J.B. offered a room at his house." And a whole lot more...

"For a fake fiancé, he sure has a hell of a nerve. Are you sleeping with him?" Jonathan's tone was truculent.

She scowled at him, long accustomed to his protective nature. "I love you, big brother. And I love my gift. But I won't have this discussion with you. Are we clear?" Some things were far too private.

"What will you tell Dad?"

"The truth. That I'm helping out a friend. I'll drop by here and see him every other day or so until he leaves. By the time he gets back from the cruise, all of this will be over."

"So you'll spend Christmas with the Vaughans? That would make me feel better about leaving you."

"Maybe so, or if that doesn't work out, maybe with Gina's crew. She has so many cousins they would never notice one more person. She's always asking me to come to family things. I don't know that Mrs. Vaughan will feel up to having much of a Christmas, anyway."

"Okay. As long as you're not alone."

"Being alone isn't so bad," she said. "It's not the same as being *lonely*. I have you and Dad and all kinds of friends. I'll be fine."

The question remained, would she spend Christmas in J.B.'s bed?

Her brave statement to Jonathan was tested a few hours later.

With the lights out and the room dark, all she could

think about was how much she wanted J.B. here beside her. The strength of that yearning was a wake-up call. How had he wormed his way into her heart so quickly?

It occurred to her that over the years she had whipped up her antipathy toward him for no other reason than to keep from admitting that she still had feelings for him. Not teenage heart palpitations, but full-blown, adult emotions that left her weak and vulnerable and afraid.

J.B. was playing with her. Not cruelly, but for fun. He was intent on having a grown-up sleepover.

A holiday affair.

She would be a fool to let him have that much control over her happiness. To let him lure her into his home and into his bed.

Even knowing every single reason that she had to guard her heart, she couldn't resist the pull of the perfect holiday with J.B.

Admitting the truth was both elating and terrifying.

Come morning, she was going to pack a bag and cast her lot with Charleston's *baddest* bachelor.

When she reached the hospital on Sunday just before noon, she was suddenly unsure about going in. J.B. hadn't called. Or texted. They had left things between them at a rather volatile crossroads last night.

Maybe he was regretting his impulsive invitation.

It wasn't too late to undo that. Her bag was in the trunk. No reason for him to ever know she had come prepared.

Because she had dropped by work briefly before coming to the hospital, she was dressed nicely in a black pencil skirt, emerald green silk blouse and her new necklace. The large pearl nestled just at the top of her cleavage.

She touched the cool stone. Jonathan understood all she had missed as a child…all they both had missed. The pearl couldn't bring her mother back, but it was a tangible link to all the might-have-beens.

Inside the hospital, she headed straight for the information desk and confirmed that Mrs. Vaughan had been moved to a regular room. That was definitely good news. When Mazie made her way upstairs, she found only Alana in residence. Even the bed was empty.

The woman who was only a couple years younger than Mazie smiled. "They took Mom one flight up for cardiac rehab. She'll be back soon."

"And the rest of your family?"

"Dad's an early riser. He got here at six this morning and sent J.B. home to sleep. Pop is downstairs grabbing a snack right now. Leila and I were here by eight. Mom's asking for her favorite coffee. The doctor okayed it, so Leila went to get her some."

"Well, it sounds like you have everything under control. Perhaps I'll swing by later in the day."

Alana hopped up, tossing the paperback book she had been reading into her tote. "Actually, I have a favor to ask."

"I'd be happy to help," Mazie said. "What is it?"

"My sister and I have matinee tickets for *The Nutcracker* at 2:00 p.m. today. Mom remembered and is insisting we go. One of the tickets was for her, so she wants Daddy to take her place. Which is stupid, because the man is *not* a ballet fan, but what can he do? He wants to make her happy."

"I'd be happy to sit with your mother," Mazie said.

"J.B. will be back soon. You wouldn't be here alone."

"I've already said yes," Mazie teased. "No need to oversell it."

"Perfect," Alana said.

At that moment, an orderly wheeled Mrs. Vaughan back into the room and helped her into bed. Mazie hovered in the hall during the transfer, not wanting to be in the way. Soon, Mr. Vaughan and his other daughter arrived, as well. The controlled chaos lasted for several minutes.

Mazie could hear J.B.'s mother directing everyone's movements. Mazie grinned to herself. No wonder the Vaughans loved and feared Jane. She was a formidable force.

At last the hoopla settled and the room quieted. Mazie could hear Jane asking for her. She stepped to the door. "I'm here."

Jane kissed her husband and daughters as they leaned over her bed. "Go have fun, my loves. Mazie and J.B. will look after me until you get back."

Soon the room emptied, and it was just Mazie and Jane. For the first time since Mazie had arrived, the older woman seemed to deflate.

"I'm toast," she grumbled. "I hate feeling this way."

"You had a major heart attack and serious surgery. It's going to take some time. Why don't you rest until they bring your lunch tray?"

"I'm tired of resting. Tell me about your family. I need distractions. I'm going crazy in this place."

Mazie pulled up a chair. "Okay. What do you remember?"

"Not much," Jane said. "When you children were

small, I knew your parents well, but the years passed, you all grew up, and we lost touch."

"You know about my mother, though?"

Jane's expression softened. "I do. The poor woman had demons, I suppose. And you were just a babe."

"Old enough to remember her leaving."

J.B.'s mother patted the bed. "Come sit here." Jane took her hand. "Everyone in Charleston knew what was happening. But the scuttlebutt was never unkind. Your parents were well respected, and to see you children lose your mother…" She shook her head, her gaze sober. "We all grieved for you and your brothers. And your father, too, of course. How is Gerald doing these days?"

"His health is precarious. He's twenty-two years older than my mom, so he's beginning to slow down."

"It must have been hard for him. Sending her away."

Mazie stood up and paced, her arms wrapped around her waist. "Yes. My brothers and I visit her occasionally. Up in Vermont. But she hasn't known us for years. She seems happy, though."

"If you marry my son, I'd be honored to be your mother-in-law."

It sounded like a joke, but when Mazie turned around and stared at her, Jane was clearly dead serious. Mazie hesitated. "You told me you understood that J.B. was inventing this whole engagement charade."

"I do. But sometimes a man does things for reasons he can't even understand until later."

"Mrs. Vaughan… Jane. Please don't set your heart on this." She bit her lip. "It's not real."

"I've seen the way he looks at you."

Mazie swallowed, desperately wanting to believe that Jane was right. "He's physically attracted to me.

For the moment. I think it's probably the thrill of the chase. As soon as I sell my property to him, he'll lose interest."

"It's time he settled down."

"J.B. has a great life. I don't think he's missing out on anything."

"And what about you, Mazie?"

Fourteen

J.B. heard just enough of the conversation in his mother's hospital room to realize that poor Mazie was floundering. He bumped the partially open door with his hip and entered. "I brought Chinese for Mazie and me. Sorry, Mom. We can eat in the lounge if it makes you too hungry."

He smothered a grin at the naked relief on Mazie's face. "Thanks, J.B."

A young woman in pink scrubs brought in the noon meal and set it on the bedside table. While J.B. set out the more appetizing of the two feasts, Mazie helped Jane get organized.

As everyone was digging in, Jane smiled genially.

"We should settle on your wedding date immediately," she pronounced, staring at her broiled codfish with distaste. "All the best summer venues will be booked soon."

J.B. took his mother's outrageous efforts in stride. He was used to her tactics.

Poor Mazie, on the other hand, choked on a bite of moo shu pork, her expression impossible to read. Her cheeks turned pink. Was she appalled or intrigued about the mention of wedded bliss?

For his part, the idea didn't bother him as much as it should have.

J.B. shook his head. "Back off, Mom. I love you, but this is between Mazie and me."

Mazie nodded. "Please don't be offended. But we're in no rush, Jane. J.B. has this big project ahead of him, and besides, we haven't been together all that long."

His mother shook her head, picking at a cup of out-of-the-can fruit cocktail. She shot a sly glance that J.B. intercepted, though he didn't think Mazie saw. "You know how much I hate downtime, son. This wedding could be the perfect thing to occupy me while I'm having to take it easy."

"Nice try, Mom. Guilt and coercion are not going to work on either of us. Mazie and I are adults. You'll have to trust us to decide when the time is right. Now eat your lunch and behave."

The remainder of the afternoon passed without fireworks. His mother napped off and on. In between, he and Mazie entertained her with lighthearted conversation about anything and everything. Mazie was great with his mom. For a woman who had grown up without a female role model, she was remarkably astute when it came to handling a difficult parent.

Caring for her father had shaped her adult life.

By the time the next shift arrived at five, J.B. was more than ready to spirit Mazie away. Watching her all afternoon had been slow torture. He wanted to make love to her again. Badly. And this time in a comfortable bed with soft sheets where he could take his time with her. The prospect dried his mouth and tightened his body.

She was an elegant woman, graceful, fun loving, and above all, kind. Which didn't explain why she had given him such grief about selling her building. The place was a mess. Heating, wiring, water issues in the basement. Everything he had offered Mazie as a trade was far and away better. But she had clung to her hatred of him. He liked to think he had mended fences with her now…that what happened so long ago no longer mattered.

Some people said love was the flip side of hate. Did he want that from Mazie? Surely not. He'd been vulnerable once, had trusted a woman. The betrayal that followed had cost him his heart, his pride and his fortune.

Mazie wasn't like his ex-wife. He'd stake his life on it.

But did he really want to take a chance?

His mother's heart attack had diverted his attention. But now that she was on the mend, he needed to focus his attention on persuading Mazie to sell.

Perhaps he could combine business with pleasure. He had asked her to spend Christmas with him. Was she going to say yes? The prospect was far more personal than he wanted to admit.

When his father and sisters shooed him on his way—after heaping gratitude on Mazie for spending her Sunday afternoon at the hospital—J.B. followed Mazie outside, breathing in the crisp evening air with a groan of relief.

"God, I hate hospitals," he said. "The smells. The sad faces. I hope Mom doesn't have to stay long."

Mazie rolled her shoulders. "It's a great hospital, J.B. But I know what you mean."

"Are you hungry?"

"Not yet."

"You want to walk the bridge?" The Ravenel Bridge, completed in 2005, had been constructed with both a pedestrian path and a bike lane. It was a popular destination any time of the year, but in December when the weather was kind, it couldn't be beat.

Mazie nodded. "I'd love to. I've been feeling like a slug." She glanced down at her slim skirt and high heels. "I'll have to put on other clothes."

They had made it out of the lobby and were standing on the sidewalk near the main parking lot. J.B. took her arm, his fingertips rubbing lightly over the narrow bones of her wrist. "Did you bring what you needed to stay over?" He felt her pulse jump.

She nodded slowly. When she lifted her gaze to his, he saw deep vulnerability. "I'm not sure why, but I did."

Exultation flooded his veins, though he kept his expression noncommittal. Words he couldn't say hovered on his lips. Words that would change everything. He couldn't do it. He wouldn't. It wasn't really necessary to upset the status quo. Too much at stake. "Good. Let's meet at my house, and we'll both get changed."

Was that disappointment he saw on her face? He felt a lick of shame, but it didn't sway him.

The distance was short, ten minutes at the most. Even so, he held his breath until he saw Mazie's distinctive car pull into his narrow driveway and squeeze in beside his SUV.

He slammed his car door and waited, rifling though his pockets for what he wanted to give her.

Mazie got out as well, with her purse slung over her shoulder and a stylish duffel in her hand.

"I made you a set of keys," he said. "I'll remind you how to use the alarm before we go to bed tonight." He took the heavy bag from her.

She wrapped her arms around her waist. "That's not really necessary, is it? I won't be here long."

"I want you to feel at home."

As he said the words, something about them set off warning bells in his head. When had he *ever* said that exact phrase to a woman? Never that he could recall.

He would have to tread carefully. Mazie might get the wrong idea. Even worse, so might he.

Inside, he led her upstairs, bypassing his bedroom and ushering her into a beautifully decorated guest room. The celadon hues were soothing.

"This is beautiful," Mazie said.

He set her bag on the dresser. "I hope you won't want to spend too much time in here."

Her mouth dropped open in a little O of shock. Hot pink color flooded her face. "J.B., I…"

He held up a hand. "It's your room. Completely private. No strings attached. But I reserve the right to remind you how sweet it is when we both give in to temptation."

She lifted an eyebrow. "Sweet? More like insane."

"So you admit it."

Mazie shrugged, her gaze moody and restless as she dropped her purse on a chair and examined the amenities.

"It would be hard not to," she muttered, running her hand over the bedspread.

Watching her touch the bed was almost tactile. His skin quivered as if she were stroking *him*. He kept his distance, though it strained every ounce of his control.

He loved her.

The admission slapped him like a jolt of cold water on a winter morning. He wanted to snatch her up and kiss her senseless and bury himself inside her until he couldn't breathe with wanting her.

But the consequences of such abandon were very nearly life and death.

He couldn't dive into this thing without remembering the past. Failure. Humiliation. Self-loathing.

Instead, he did the mature, nonreckless thing. "Get dressed," he said gruffly. "We'll walk the bridge, and then I'll take you for fresh shrimp and hush puppies at Lolita's."

This time, Mazie's smile was open and untinged with the wariness that was so much a part of her personality.

"For that kind of positive reinforcement, I'll follow you anywhere."

J.B. needed exercise. Badly.

And though he would have preferred the kind between the sheets, it was probably better this way.

Mazie changed clothes as quickly as he did. Soon they were on their way toward the bridge. Beneath the magnificent structure with the two triangular sets of silvery spires, an enterprising city had installed parking and a labyrinth of short trails.

While Mazie hopped out and began stretching, J.B.

locked the car and tried not to look at the way black spandex cupped her cute butt. Lord help him. He did a few stretches, too, but he was antsy. "Let's go," he said. "We can walk the first quarter mile to warm up."

They were far from the only people enjoying the bridge. Though the sounds of cars whizzing by a few feet away on the other side of the concrete barrier was not exactly relaxing, being able to look down on the city of Charleston made up for it. They started out at a brisk walk.

When Mazie shed her jacket and tied it around her waist, he gave her a nod. "Ready?"

"Yep. I'll drop back when people pass us."

They set off at an easy jog. Tension winnowed away from his body step by step. For weeks he had been totally immersed in the huge project that included Mazie's shop. And then the scare with his mother had left their entire family on edge.

But the emotions that had truly kept him tied in knots day and night were all because of Mazie.

At the top of the arc, he expected her to stop, but she kept on running, her ponytail bouncing in the wind. He kept pace with her, curbing his stride to match hers. At the other end, they did an about-face and headed back. This time, when they hit dead center on the bridge, Mazie paused long enough to stare down into the inky black Cooper River far below.

On sunny, bright days, you could spot dolphins frolicking. Tonight, the deep water was mysterious.

He bumped her hip with his. "We can't stand here too long, or we'll get cold. And I'm starving."

A smile curved her mouth. "Have you ever heard of delayed gratification?"

He took her arm. "Not a fan."

They walked quickly, using the last segment to lower their heart rates. Unfortunately, being near Mazie kept his blood pressure and respiration perpetually in the red zone.

For the moment, he would sublimate with food.

Lolita's was a hole-in-wall place. The kind of eatery the locals patronized and tourists rarely took the time to find. Not on the beach, but near enough the water to have the best seafood in Mount Pleasant.

Even better, the ambiance was definitely casual. He and Mazie didn't look out of place in their running clothes.

The hostess led them to a scarred table beneath a huge stuffed tarpon wearing a Santa hat. She handed them plastic-coated menus. "Wreckfish is the special tonight. Two sides. Thirty-five bucks. It's worth the price. Soup of the day is seafood gumbo. Let me grab you a couple of waters, and I'll be back to take your order."

Mazie yawned. "Sorry," she said as the waitress walked away. "I didn't sleep great last night. Jonathan and I had eggs and bacon late, and I drank half a cup of coffee. I was able to do that in college, but I guess I'm getting old."

J.B. leaned back in his chair and chuckled. "Yeah. You're ancient." He glanced around the restaurant, noting the multiple strands of Christmas lights and the ubiquitous tinsel garlands. "I suppose I should confess something. My housekeeper decorated my place for the holidays. Garlands and lights and such. But I don't have a tree. Seems kind of a waste for just me."

"No worries," she said. "We never have a tree up at our house."

He frowned. "You're kidding. I thought you were the one who loved Christmas. Jonathan jokes about it and how he has to hide his Scroogish tendencies when you're around."

"I do love Christmas," she said. "But we haven't decorated since my mom left. At first, we kids were too little, and by the time we were in high school, the moment had passed. The boys weren't particularly interested, and I was self-conscious about tackling it on my own. Plus, I was afraid it would make my father sad. So we don't deck the halls." She shrugged. "There are enough decorations elsewhere for me to enjoy. It's no big deal."

But it was a big deal. He hated the thought of a little girl yearning for candles and ornaments and wreaths and a tree and having no one to get them for her.

Their meal arrived. Both of them cleaned their plates.

Mazie finished her last plump shrimp and her last crispy hush puppy. "This place is amazing. I'm glad you thought of it."

The blissful appreciation on her face was aimed at the food, but J.B. was equally willing to accommodate any other appetites she might have. His body ached for her. The urgency of his desire was outrageous enough to slow him down for a moment.

Though he would like to take her straight back to the house and strip her naked, he needed to take a deep breath and get some perspective. Besides, she needed some pampering.

After taking care of the check, he ushered her outside. "I have a surprise," he said.

As usual, Mazie's response was laced with suspicion. "I hope it doesn't involve bank vaults."

Was she flirting with him? Or simply giving him a hard time? It baffled him that he still had difficulty understanding her. Usually he could read people like open books. Mazie was a whole damned library with the doors padlocked.

He opened the car door for her and tried to help her up into the passenger seat, but she waved him away. "I can do it."

"Fine," he muttered. He waited until she was settled and slammed the door. Loping around to the driver's side, he quickly composed and discarded several versions of a plan to make her smile.

It was Christmas. The season of peace and goodwill. He and Mazie were mending fences, but he wanted more. He was tired of living in the shadows of his own failures.

Suddenly, he knew he had to give her the perfect, special holiday.

For a split second, he envisioned a year in the future with the two of them gathered around a fireplace reading books to a toddler. The image shocked him so much, he almost ran a red light. Tonight was about Mazie's broken childhood. He didn't want to examine his other motives too closely.

Mazie shot him a glance. "You okay?"

He swallowed the lump in his throat. "Yeah. Sorry. My mind was on something else."

She patted his thigh. "I understand. You must be so worried about your mom. But she's doing well, J.B.

Honestly, she is. When you all were gone today, she told me she's feeling stronger every day."

"Yeah, I know." His mother was definitely on his mind. But her condition was stable. This thing with Mazie was definitely *not* stable.

Up ahead, he finally spotted what he was looking for. He turned into a parking lot and shut off the engine.

Mazie looked through the windshield and then sideways at him. "What are we doing here?"

"What do you think?" He reached across the small space between them and caressed her cheek with the pad of his thumb. "I think you've been a very good girl this year. Santa wants you to have all the trimmings."

Fifteen

Mazie's throat tightened. Tears stung her eyes. How dumb was this? She surely wasn't going to get all emotional because a man was being sweet and kind and indulging her love of the holiday.

J.B. stared at her with a quizzical smile on his face. He had charisma in spades. No wonder he'd dated his way through half the women in Charleston. He was a young George Clooney. Charming. Funny. Hard to pin down.

"Are you sure?" she asked. "Real Christmas trees shed needles everywhere. And they can be hard to set up."

J.B. grinned. "Challenge accepted."

"Okay, then. You asked for it."

She hopped out of the car and inhaled a deep lungful of balsam-scented air. "Take a whiff," she said. "No artificial tree can give you this."

Though it had been dark now for several hours, the proprietor had strung up long swaths of colored lights among his offerings. Christmas carols played in the background from an old-fashioned boom box. Because it was getting closer to the main event, the Christmas-tree lot was crowded with browsers.

Moms and dads and excited children. Young couples. Families with teenagers.

For a split second, Mazie felt like a child again with all the anticipation and wonder and hope of innocence. And she owed it all to the man who had once broken her heart. But he had changed, she was sure of it. And now his sensual charm was irresistible.

J.B. tagged along behind her with an indulgent smile on his face as she walked through the rows of freshly cut trees. Half a dozen varieties were represented, but the Fraser firs were her favorites.

She bypassed the six- and seven-foot trees and headed for the bigger ones. J.B.'s living room had high ceilings. No need to skimp.

At her request, he held up one tree at a time, twirling them around so Mazie could inspect all sides. Finally, she found the one she wanted. It was perfectly symmetrical, and it was fat and healthy. It topped J.B. by almost two feet.

For the first time, he winced. "You sure about this? It's gonna look bigger when we get it inside."

"It's the perfect tree," she said. "You'll see."

While J.B. paid for the expensive fir, and the man tucked it in a mesh sleeve for the trip home, Mazie gave herself a stern lecture. She would *not* let herself be sucked into a fantasy where J.B. doted on her and actually cared about her. Everything about this weird December aberration was make-believe.

He liked having sex with her. And maybe he was also stringing her along so she would sell him her property, or he was worried about his mother and using Mazie's sympathetic heart to help him get through these difficult days, or both.

That was all this was.

At the moment, he looked like a ruggedly sexy lumberjack. He had hefted the heavy tree on top of the car, and was now securing it with bungees.

She joined him and slid an arm around his waist, feeling his muscles strain as he worked.

"You're my hero," she said, only half joking.

He stepped back and wiped sap from his forehead. "You owe me for this. Just so you know, I plan to collect later tonight."

His wicked grin curled her toes. "The tree was your idea," she pointed out, leaning into him and inhaling the scent of warm male. "I merely went along with the adventure."

"Smart woman." He kissed her nose and then found her mouth with his. The second kiss started out lazy for five seconds and then hardened.

Mazie arched her neck, kissing him back. "You drive me crazy," she muttered.

"The feeling is mutual." He backed her against the side of the car, his lower body pinning hers to the vehicle. "I haven't needed anyone like this in a very long time. You make me want to be sixteen again."

"No," she groaned, her arms tightening around his neck. "Not that. I want the J.B. who knows all the naughty secrets about women."

He pulled back, his gaze oddly abashed and serious for the moment. "I don't know all *your* secrets, Mazie."

"I don't have anything to hide," she said lightly. The lie was both easy and disturbing.

He sucked in a sharp breath, his chest heaving, as he looked around at all the people keeping them from a private moment. "We still have to buy decorations," he muttered.

"Then let's go."

They hit up a fancy department store nearby, cleaning out a huge percentage of their handblown ornaments and silvery tinsel. Mazie added box after box of multicolored lights to the haul.

When the cashier rang up the total, J.B. never flinched. He handed over his platinum card and scrawled his name on the credit slip, giving the poor woman a smile that made her blush from her throat to her hairline, though she was old enough to be his grandmother.

Mazie rolled her eyes. The man couldn't help himself. His masculinity was electric and compelling.

Back in the car, she yawned. "It's probably too late to decorate tonight."

"I hope that means what I think it means."

She fidgeted in her seat, trying to get comfortable, her breath coming faster. "I could be persuaded."

"Oh, no," he said, staring at the traffic and not at her, so that she saw only his profile. "You're a guest in my home. I'll need a firm, unequivocal invitation."

There was a tongue-in-cheek tone to his voice, but what he said made sense. It would be cowardly on Mazie's part to pretend reluctance when the truth was, she wanted him every bit as badly as he wanted her.

Sliding her hand across the leather bench seat, she placed it on his upper thigh, gripping the taut muscle beneath his pants. "I'd like to have sex with you, J.B. In a bed, in a chair, heck, even in your fancy kitchen." She sighed. "You're a very tempting man. And I'm in a mood to indulge."

He shot her a sideways glance. "You sound like someone prepared to go off a diet. Am I really that bad for you?"

She pretended to mull it over. "Hmm. Let me see. A commitment-phobic bachelor. A relationship that will possibly hurt other people when it ends, including me. That's a yes, J.B. I don't think you're my smartest choice, but I'm not going to run away. You're exactly what I want for Christmas."

They were parked in his narrow driveway now, with two houses looming on either side. The vehicle was dark. What was he thinking? Had she startled him with her plain speaking?

After a long, tense silence, he handed her his keys. "Unlock the front door. I'll carry the tree in."

She did as he requested, and then stood aside while he brought the large Fraser fir into the house. Immediately, the foyer filled with the fragrance of outdoors. Crisp, clean. If they invented a name for this particular scent, Mazie would call it *mountain morning*.

They had bought a tree stand, a fancy one that held a good supply of water but could be tilted carefully to straighten the trunk. Somehow, they had to unwrap the tree, lift it into the container and tighten the bolts.

Suddenly, Mazie realized that she should be the one to call the shots. J.B. was trying to give her a Christmas experience she had missed for many years. He wouldn't stop until the whole damn tree was ablaze with lights and sparkling with expensive ornaments.

After he leaned the tree in a corner and dusted off his hands, she went to him and laid her head on his shoulder. "I'm serious. I don't want to decorate this tree tonight."

She felt his body tense. "You're sure?"

"I'd rather decorate you. Maybe a dab of whipping cream. A little chocolate. What do you say?"

His laugh sounded breathless. "Don't toy with me, woman."

It came to her in that moment that she was in over her head. She had wanted him forever, it seemed. But for years, she had been afraid to admit those feelings or to fight for what she needed and deserved.

In spite of the risks, she was all in now. When it came to a choice, she would always choose J.B. Maybe the aftermath of this little experiment was going to suck, but that was in the future. For now, she wanted him so much it left her breathless.

"No games," she whispered. "But I think I'd like a quick shower first."

He grabbed her hand and dragged her toward the stairs. "We'll do it together and save time."

"I can't remember if I shaved my legs."

"Doesn't matter."

His desperation might have been flattering if she hadn't been so scared of letting him know how she felt. She had to keep this light and physical. No messy emotional connection.

That was hard to do when he was so damned cute.

In his bathroom, he released her only long enough to turn on the water in the shower enclosure and adjust the temperature. When he turned around, Mazie was naked from the waist up.

His cheeks flushed dark red. "I think you're getting ahead of me," he croaked.

"Maybe you should try harder." She stripped his shirt over his head and kissed his nipples. They were flat and copper colored, and he hissed with pleasure when she licked them.

His running pants were thin nylon. They did little to disguise the fact that his sex was rising to the occasion rapidly, thick and eager.

By unspoken consent, they each removed the remainder of their own clothes. She was bashful, but not reluctant. The look in J.B.'s eyes made a woman feel invincible.

When they were both completely nude, he took her hand, lifted it to his lips and kissed her fingers. "After you, my lady."

Her hair was in a knot on top of her head, because they had been running earlier, so she didn't have to worry about putting it up. It would be easy enough not to get it wet. At least that's what she thought until J.B. joined her.

Even though his hedonistic shower was huge, the guy was big. He took up a lot of room.

Mazie backed against the corner, her heart beating far too fast.

"Face the other wall," she said. "I'll wash your back." Anything to keep him from staring at her. When he turned away, she breathed a sigh of relief.

With shaking hands, she picked up the washcloth

and soaped it. Then she started at the back of his neck and rubbed hard enough to make his skin pink. Next, his shoulders, his broad back and his narrow waist.

J.B. groaned as if she was torturing him…when all she was doing was playing the role of a bathhouse girl. She kneeled on the slick floor and soaped the backs of his legs…powerful thighs, muscular calves. Even his bare feet were sexy. Now that it was time for him to turn around, she nearly lost her nerve.

She rose to her feet and put both hands on his shoulders. "All done here."

He spun slowly and stared at her. The heat in his blue-eyed gaze made her stomach clench with desire. "You gonna wash the rest of me?" he asked, a tiny smile tipping the corners of his mouth.

"I think you're perfectly capable of handling that," she said primly.

"Then I'll do *your* back. You know…tit for tat."

She tried not to laugh. "I don't believe that word is politically correct anymore."

He lifted an eyebrow. "Tat?"

"You're impossible."

He put his wet hands on her shoulders and turned her away from him. Soon, the feel of his hands on her body made her legs shaky. Especially when one particular part of *him* kept bumping her bottom.

J.B. put a lot of effort into making sure she was clean from head to toe. He seemed particularly taken with her bottom. When he had soaped it up to his liking, he rested his erection in the cleft and slowly massaged her with his sex.

Oh, lordy.

He'd barely gotten started, and she was falling apart.

"J.B.?"

"Hmm?" He kissed the back of her neck, nibbling gently.

"We're using an awful lot of water. Seems irresponsible."

Without warning, his arms came around her from behind. "Let me finish this one part," he muttered. "Then we'll get out."

He abandoned the washcloth. Instead, his big soapy hands caressed her breasts.

Her head fell back against his shoulder. "I don't think my boobs are all that dirty," she panted, trying not to beg him to take her then and there.

"Maybe not." He tweaked her sensitive nipples. "But they're so damned pretty when they're wet and slick."

She was wet and slick somewhere else. Embarrassingly so. But it seemed rude to mention it. Not when J.B. was doing such a bang-up job of bathing her. His hands were gentle and thorough. Much more of this and she would melt…maybe slide right down the drain.

When the water started to run cold, she seized the chance to move their interlude to somewhere less wet and more horizontal. After all, she didn't want to be responsible for either one of them cracking their skull in the shower.

"Bed," she begged. "Let's get in your bed. The water is freezing."

J.B. couldn't argue with that. He turned off the faucet and grabbed towels for both of them. "Your lips are blue," he said. "Poor baby. I'll have to warm them up."

She scrubbed her body with the dry towel and

grabbed a robe off the back of the door. "Meet you on the mattress. Bring condoms."

He followed her, pausing only to rummage in a bathroom drawer. "Plural," he teased. "I like how you think."

J.B.'s bed was a testament to fine linens and the ingenuity of an American mattress company. She climbed beneath the covers, tossed her damp towel on the floor and reveled in the unmistakable luxury of thousand-thread-count sheets. It figured that J.B. would have only the best in his bachelor paradise.

Instead of joining her immediately, he stood with his hands on his hips and stared at her.

Mazie clutched the covers to her chin. "I thought you'd be in more of a hurry." The part of him that reared strong and proud against his flat belly seemed not inclined to wait.

One masculine shoulder lifted and fell. "I'm enjoying the prelude," he said, the words low and husky. "You look delicious in my bed."

"Like an apple waiting to be picked?"

"Like a moment I want to paint and record for posterity."

The sappy romantic comment stunned her. Not because he said it jokingly, but because of the utter sincerity in his quiet words.

"I want you here with me," she begged. "Come warm me up." His steady regard made her self-conscious.

He dropped the towel wrapped around his hips. "I can do that."

When he joined her underneath the covers, something inside her sighed with contentment. Which was odd, because she was a long way from satisfied.

She ran her hand down his flank. Questions trembled on her lips. Requests for reassurance. Demands about the future.

What did J.B. want from her? Was any of this more than a lark for him?

Swallowing her uncertainties was much harder than it should have been.

"Thank you for the Christmas tree," she said.

He turned on his side and faced her, resting his head on his hand. This close she could see his thick eyelashes and the sparkles of gold in his blue irises.

"I'm glad we skipped decorating for this instead," he said.

Despite her best efforts, her insecurity slipped out. "What is *this*, J.B.?"

The faint frown on his face told her she had overstepped some invisible boundary. "Do we have to ask that question right now? Can't we enjoy the moment?"

She nodded slowly, swallowing her disappointment. "Of course we can."

Hurt bubbled in her chest, but she ignored it.

J.B. wasn't a forever kind of man. She had known that when she climbed into his bed. She would take this temporary affair and wallow in the magic of Christmas. Reality was something that could wait for the cold, bleak days of January.

"Make love to me," she whispered.

Her words galvanized him. Bending over her, he suckled her breasts and slid a hand between her thighs. When he entered her with his finger, she cried out. Her body was taut with arousal.

A lock of his hair fell over his forehead. His face

was flushed. "I want you, Mazie Jane. Insanely, as it happens. Why do you think that is?"

"Maybe you got tired of women who won't stand up to you."

He choked out a laugh, as if her blunt honesty had surprised him. "You're prickly and unpredictable. I've had easier women, that's for sure."

When she reached for his erection, he batted her hand away. "Next time, love. I'm too primed for that." He sheathed himself and moved on top of her, fitting the blunt head of his sex at her entrance. "Lift your arms," he demanded. "Hold on to the headboard."

She obeyed automatically, clenching her fingers tightly around the wavy iron bars. Her eyelids fluttered shut.

J.B. pushed inside her slowly. The feeling was indescribable. She heard a ragged curse, as if he, too, was surprised at the way their bodies fit together. Yin and yang. As old as time. As new and fragile and precious as a morning mist on the beach.

"Open your eyes, sweet girl. Don't hide from me."

She tried. The intimacy was painful. His features were taut, his expression impossible to read.

But she, on the other hand, felt naked. Surely he could see everything she had hidden for so long. Her wrists weren't immobilized. She could have touched him if she wanted.

Still, she didn't move. She held her breath, her body straining against his, her heart soaking up every tender, muttered endearment, every rough thrust, every unbelievably raw emotion.

"J.B.," she cried out, feeling the peak rush toward her.

He buried his face in her hot neck. "Come for me, Mazie."

She wrapped her arms around him, arched her back and obeyed...

Sixteen

Mazie had never enjoyed *sleeping* with a man. Actually *sleeping*. But somehow, curling up with J.B. and letting drowsiness roll over her was the most wonderful feeling in the world.

By the time she awoke the next morning, something had changed. Not in him, maybe, but in her. No matter how foolish or self-destructive, she had to admit the truth.

She had fallen in love with J.B.

There hadn't been far to fall. Deep in a sixteen-year-old girl's heart the memory of her feelings for him had lived on, just as strongly as the memory of her mother's leaving home when she was twelve.

Traumatic events, world-changing events, never really went away. A person just learned to bury them. She had covered her desire for J.B. with animosity, trying to pretend he was nothing to her. It had worked for a long time—years even. But no more.

The covers were warm. J.B.'s big body was warm. He held her cradled in his arms, her head on his shoulder.

What was she going to do? How far could she let herself be pulled into his orbit and still be able to break free?

He stirred and gave her a sleepy smile. "Hey, there, gorgeous."

She cupped his stubbly chin. "Shouldn't you be at work?"

J.B. yawned and glanced at the digital clock on the bedside table. "I've got it covered."

"What does that mean?"

"Isn't All That Glitters closed on Mondays?"

She was surprised he had paid that much attention. "Yes."

He kissed her nose. "I wanted to spend the day with you. My partner is on call for any emergencies. It's almost Christmas. Things are slow."

It bothered her that he hadn't said a word about their long-standing feud or her property or his big project that included her. After his mother's heart attack, he had backed off completely. Two weeks ago, his Realtor had been contacting Mazie every three or four days. Now, nothing.

Was J.B. playing a game with her? Did he think she would cooperate if he wrapped her in romance and soft sheets?

Once before, she had been positive he had feelings for her. When the teenage J.B. had exhibited arousal, she'd been naive enough to believe it was going to lead to something. To a relationship. To a future.

He had disabused her of that notion cruelly.

Was she courting heartbreak a second time? Was J.B. even capable of love? Did he want more than her body and her business?

Was J.B. Vaughan her soul mate or her worst nightmare?

She wanted to take this experience at face value. She wanted to live in the moment. Sadly, she had never been the kind of woman to enjoy sex for the sake of sex. Before this thing with J.B., she had been celibate for two years.

"What did you have in mind?" she asked, snuggling closer.

His eyes were heavy-lidded, his hair tousled. Without his fancy suits and his billionaire persona, he looked far more dangerous.

"I thought after breakfast we could decorate the tree," he said. "Then take a shift at the hospital sitting with Mom."

"I like it."

"But first…" He reached for a foil packet on the nightstand and turned back to press a possessive kiss on her mouth. "I want to play."

After last night's excess, this morning should have been lazy and indulgent. Instead, it was as if the world was ending and this was their last chance to find a mate.

J.B. touched her everywhere, whispering her name, showering her with endearments and compliments. Her first climax hit sharp and hard and left her shaking. Before she could do more than gasp for breath, he was driving her up again…raking her nipples with sharp teeth, pressing kisses to her belly and below. Filling her with his powerful thrusts.

When she came a second time, he was there with her, a muffled shout buried against her throat. She wrapped her legs around his waist and held him tightly, her eyes damp.

They slept again.

When she woke up the next time, her stomach was growling.

"Feed me," she begged, shaking his shoulder.

J.B. rolled out of bed and padded to the bathroom, giving her a tantalizing view of his male beauty. "You're so demanding."

She could hear his laughter, even after he closed the door.

While J.B. was getting dressed, she took a quick shower, fetched her bag from the guest room, and pulled out fresh clothes. It sounded like the day would be casual, which suited her just fine. Mondays were usually lazy days, her one indulgence in a week that was typically crammed with work and looking after her father.

She followed her nose to the kitchen and found J.B. knee deep in eggs and bacon.

"Shall I make toast?" she asked, pausing to lean her cheek against his arm.

He gave her a quick kiss. "Butter's on the counter right behind me. There's a loaf of bread in the pantry. Coffee's ready if you want some."

The homey scene was entirely bogus. J.B. Vaughan was not a domesticated animal. Mazie didn't even want to calculate the number of women who had wandered into this charming kitchen scene over the years.

She knew this wasn't the same place J.B. lived during his short marriage. That knowledge should have made her feel better. And it did…a tiny bit. Truthfully, she adored his carefully preserved row house.

The copper-bottomed pots hanging over the island might be only for show, but as far as she could tell, J.B.'s kitchen was outfitted like a chef's dream. Mazie liked to cook when she had the time. It wasn't hard to imagine herself right here in the midst of preparing a big dinner for a group of friends.

While J.B. scrambled and fried, she found a cookie sheet and decided to do the toast in the oven. When it was done, she joined him at the table and slid two pieces of perfectly browned sourdough onto each plate.

A jar of homemade plum preserves she had found in the fridge was the finishing touch.

J.B. devoured the meal as if he were starving.

Truth be told, they had expended a great deal of energy since they ate shrimp the night before. And it was already midmorning.

She reached across the table and removed a drop of jam from his chin. "How are you at putting Christmas lights on a tree?" She vowed to keep the day light and easy. No more personal questions that would make both of them uneasy.

He finished the last bite of eggs and sat back in his chair. "Don't know. I guess we'll find out."

J.B. was in trouble.

And he knew it.

Part of him wanted to get Mazie out of his house

and out of his bed. It was beginning to feel as if she *belonged* here.

That wasn't possible.

He liked her. A lot. Still, he had done the marriage thing, and he was really bad at it. So he needed to put a stop to this *playing house* gig.

As the morning progressed, he watched her, searching for any sign that she thought this was leading to something bigger. Other than a single, logically female question last night, she hadn't pressed for answers. Maybe because he had shut her down.

He felt bad about that.

By the time they finished the tree, his living room was a mess, but Mazie was glowing. She stood back and put her hands on her hips. "Look at it, J.B. It's glorious." She threw her arms around him in a big bear hug. "I can't wait until it's dark tonight, and we get the full effect."

Her enthusiasm was contagious. He felt a sense of pride that he had been able to give her something so simple and yet so profound. Mazie was a confident, happy, successful woman, but deep inside was that sad little girl who had lost her mother and had spent multiple Christmases on the edges of someone else's celebrations.

Damn Jonathan and Hartley for not noticing. Maybe they were too close to the situation, and maybe they had other interests. It was women who usually created the warmth of holidays, women who knew how to make an occasion memorable.

But J.B. wished her family hadn't dropped the ball where Mazie was concerned.

He tugged her ponytail. "I can't wait until dark either."

She headed for the stairs. "We need to leave for the hospital. You promised we'd be there at one."

He followed her a moment later, only to find that she had taken her overnight bag and all her things to the guest room to get ready.

Why, damn it? And why wasn't he glad? He felt like he was losing his grip. Nothing made sense.

At the hospital, the news was not quite as upbeat as it had been. His mother was wan and listless. According the doctor, there was infection somewhere in her body. They were pumping her full of antibiotics.

Only Leila was there.

His sister stepped out into the hall to speak to them. "I'm not sure what happened overnight, but she was like this when I got here this morning. Dad is a wreck. I sent him home to sleep. Alana is with him."

J.B. hugged his sister. "You go, too. Mazie and I can be here as long as we need to be."

The afternoon crawled by. His mother alternated between resting and waking, barely speaking at all. Mazie sat beside her and rubbed her hand, the one that wasn't encumbered with the IV.

J.B. paced.

At one point, when their patient was sleeping, he pulled Mazie to a far corner of the room. "I feel like we should be doing something."

She grimaced. "Hospitals are all about waiting. They must think the medicine will work eventually. She's not getting worse."

He pressed the heel of his hand to his forehead. "I hate being helpless."

Mazie wrapped her arms around him. "Whatever happens, she knows how much you love her. That's the important thing."

His blood chilled. Mazie was obliquely referencing what all of them had been thinking. Jane Vaughan might not pull through this. His heart pounded and his knees felt funny. He loved his mom.

For the first time, he truly understood how Mazie must have suffered when her mom was taken away. It would have been like a death.

"I'm sorry," he said, his hands on her shoulders.

"For what?"

"For not realizing how much it has hurt you to have your mother several hundred miles away."

Mazie paled. "She doesn't even know who I am."

"So you feel guilty if you don't go and even sadder when you *do*? That's the worst of it, isn't it? You want to believe that it will be different every time you visit, but it never is."

She nodded slowly. Tears welled into her eyes and spilled onto her cheeks.

He held her close, his heart expanding with an emotion that confused him. Being so close kindled a spark of sexual arousal, but it wasn't only that. He wanted to protect her and make her happy and give her the family she had always wanted. Holy hell. What was he thinking?

Before he could make himself release her, Mazie slipped free of his arms. "Excuse me," she muttered. "I'll be back."

When he turned around, his mother's eyes were open. "You love her, don't you, son?"

He started to deny it, but at the last moment remembered the faux engagement. "Of course I do, Mom." He pulled up a chair beside the bed and studied the machines beeping softly. "How are you feeling?"

She pursed her lips. "Tired. Glad to be alive."

"I don't want you to fret. Can I go get you a hamburger? Medium rare with onions?"

The little joke made his mother smile. "You would do it, wouldn't you?"

"If you asked me. I love you, Mama."

His heart was cracking inside his chest. Breaking wide open. Between his fear for his mother and his need for Mazie, he was turning into someone he didn't recognize.

His mother put her hand on his head, almost like a blessing. "You don't have to worry about me, J.B. I'm going to live to see those grandbabies you promised me."

Guilt choked him. He couldn't tell her the truth. Not now.

Mazie returned at that moment, rescuing him from the need to deal with his mother's loaded statement. His fiancée was pale, but she seemed calm. She had been to the hospital gift shop by the looks of it. In her hand, she carried a vase of pink sweetheart roses.

"Alana told me these were your favorites."

His mother perked up visibly. "Oh, thank you, sweet girl. They're beautiful. Set them right there where I can see them."

J.B. stood. "I'm gonna grab some coffee." He was suffocating. He *wanted* Mazie here. Of course he did. But seeing her interact with his mother signaled an intimacy he was trying his damnedest to avoid.

* * *

After that particular Monday, the days fell into a pattern. Christmas was barely over a week away. J.B. and Mazie both went to work every morning, but the evenings were for taking care of family, and later for making love beneath the beautiful, fragrant Christmas tree.

J.B. had discovered Mazie's particular fantasy when it came to holiday sex, so he capitalized on it.

She had no complaints.

It was the happiest she had ever been.

Still, hovering in the back of her mind was the knowledge that she would have to leave eventually. The longer she stayed, the harder it would be to extricate herself from a relationship that was definitely lopsided when it came to the emotional component.

J.B. gave her his passion and his compassion, but his heart wasn't up for grabs.

It hurt. Badly. She couldn't lie to herself. She tried not to think about it, but deep down was a tiny stupid glimmer of hope that he would come around…that he would feel what she felt.

Because he never said the words, neither did she.

On December 22, she was so glad she had not.

It was an ordinary day, nothing to indicate that her bubble of perfect joy was about to pop.

On that morning, it was raining. J.B. kissed her goodbye as she left for work. She was wearing a black raincoat with a hood, so she thought it would be enough to keep her dry. When she got outside, though, she realized that the light showers had turned into a downpour. Not only that, she had forgotten to pick up her umbrella.

She was running late, but she scooted back inside to grab it.

As she did, she heard J.B. on the phone talking to someone. He must have been in the den, because his voice carried clearly to the foyer.

"I don't think we have anything to worry about. I've got her eating out of my hand. It won't be a problem."

All the blood drained from her heart to the floor. Numbly, she grabbed the umbrella, backed out of the house and fled.

Unfortunately, it wasn't far to her destination. She parked and gripped the steering wheel. Her mind was blank one minute and filled with pain and terror the next. Surely it couldn't be true. Surely J.B. hadn't moved her into his house and slept with her so she would give him a stupid building.

She had noticed him pulling back emotionally over the last few days. Though they had been as close as a man and woman could be from a physical standpoint, it was if J.B. had put up a mental wall between them.

She had assumed, had hoped actually, that it was because his feelings for her were changing. That maybe he was fighting the connection between them.

He had failed at commitment and marriage in the past and was too afraid to try again.

But what if his retreat was more sinister? What if he was getting ready to reject her again now that he had accomplished his goals?

Try as she might, she couldn't think of another interpretation for his words. Especially because he had sounded happy and upbeat.

With his mom on the mend and Mazie no longer a problem, he was going to have a very merry Christmas.

Mazie couldn't bear it. Why did no one she cared about stick around for the long haul?

What was wrong with her?

Seventeen

Somehow, she made it through the day.

Gina looked at her oddly several times, but they were too busy with customers for her to grill Mazie. With only two shopping days left after this one, the store was a madhouse.

Jewelry flew out the door like fake gold doubloons being tossed in a Mardi Gras parade. Fake doubloons. Like everything else in Mazie's life at the moment. Her engagement, her blackhearted lover. Even her smile. Because inside, she was nothing but a child crying in the driveway when everything she loved best was being taken away from her.

At last, the interminable day was over. She had to figure out a way to extricate herself from J.B.'s house. First, though, she had to go by the hospital. Jane was doing much better, but she wasn't entirely out of the woods.

Mazie knew J.B. was working late, so she wouldn't have to see him. Please God, let that be so.

Both Alana and Leila were with their mother. Mr. Vaughan had been home napping during the afternoon but was due back soon.

The three women in the room greeted her warmly. Mazie hung her purse on a chair and cleaned her hands with hand sanitizer.

"How's our patient today?" she asked.

Jane wagged a finger at her two daughters. "If these two will quit worrying, we'll be fine." But J.B.'s mother didn't look healthy. If anything, she seemed frail and pale.

Alana spoke up, looking chagrined. "You're not as well as you think, Mama."

"Oh, pooh. I'm determined to be home for Christmas. You wait and see."

Leila grimaced. Mazie sympathized. Jane wasn't a bad patient, but she was strong willed.

Leila hugged Mazie unexpectedly. "You've been so great to our mother. She told us that you're not actually engaged to my brother. So you've really gone above and beyond. Thank you, Mazie."

Alana hugged her, too. "I was disappointed. I think he needs someone like you in his life, but the guy is stubborn as a rock."

"Don't I know it," Mazie said lightly.

The lump in her throat was more of a boulder. Though the Vaughans didn't realize it, this was Mazie's goodbye visit. She had agreed to J.B.'s charade when she thought something real might grow out of it...when she had trusted him. Now, though, she had to leave him.

Without warning, the door swung open and J.B.

strode into the room. He carried with him the crisp masculine scent that was like a drug to her. She put the width of the bed between them and barely acknowledged his presence.

It wasn't so hard. He was chatting with his sisters and sitting on his mother's bed to speak with her.

Suddenly, every alarm in the room began to beep. Jane's eyes fluttered shut and her breathing was raspy. In an instant, three nurses ran into the room and surrounded the bed.

The three siblings clung to each other, ashen faced.

Mazie huddled in the corner, out of the way.

J.B. was wild-eyed as if he couldn't believe what was happening. He looked for Mazie.

"Come where she can hear you," he begged. "Tell her she has to hold on."

Mazie didn't know if he was asking for himself or his mother or both. But she would do whatever he asked, because she loved him desperately.

Before Mazie could move closer, Leila, tears streaming down her cheeks, patted her brother's arm. "Stop, J.B. Quit pretending. It doesn't matter now. Mom knows the engagement isn't real."

His jaw dropped. He stared at Mazie with hot eyes. "You told her?"

Humiliation burned her cheeks. "Well, I…"

His face was stony, his gaze both judge and jury. "We'll talk about this later."

A doctor joined the fray. "I'll need all of you to step into the hall, please." As a team of medical professionals swooped in, J.B. and his sisters and Mazie were kindly but firmly evicted.

J.B. took her arm and steered her a short distance away, far enough for the two of them to speak in private.

His expression was tight with fury. His grasp was firm enough to leave bruises. "Go home," he said. "I have to concentrate on my family now. They are all that matters to me."

The intimation was sharply painful. He blamed Mazie.

This wasn't the time to exonerate herself. And besides. What was the point? It didn't matter what J.B. thought of her. Their relationship—if you could call it that—was over. And this time the pain of his rejection was far more devastating than she could have imagined.

She stumbled her way to the parking lot and got into her car. Driving to J.B.'s house, dealing with the alarm, and unlocking the door took all the courage she had, even knowing that he was not going to interrupt her.

With shaking hands and a stomach curling with nausea, she packed up her clothing and personal items. Most of it was in the master bedroom. A few things in the guest room. There wasn't a lot, really.

Her holiday affair hadn't lasted all that long.

Back downstairs, she went into the den and plugged in the lights on the Christmas tree. The beautiful fir mocked her. The tears came then, hot and painful. She had gambled and lost.

J.B. hadn't cared about her when she was sixteen, and he didn't care about her now.

She was a means to an end.

When she was calm enough to drive, she headed for home. For the last week, Jonathan had been working like a madman, preparing to be gone, so he was keeping late hours. Her father was distracted with chores for his trip and would be leaving in the morning. He was the most animated she had seen him in months.

Mazie had dinner with her father and helped him pack afterward. As she was folding a pair of socks, she blurted out a question she had wanted to ask him for years but had never had the guts.

"Daddy?"

"Hmm?"

"Why do you never go see Mama? Why did you send her so very far away?"

He turned slowly, his face paling. He sat down hard on the side of the bed. "I wondered when one of you kids would finally ask me that." His voice rasped with emotion.

"I don't want to upset you, but I need to know."

He shrugged, playing with a loose thread on one of his sweaters. "When your mother had her complete psychotic break, I took her to the best and most expensive doctors in the country. Your mother was the love of my life. When she came to me, she was young and charming and so full of animation. It was only after we married that I discovered her demons."

"And nothing helped?"

"No. Not really." His jaw worked. "We went through months and years of diagnosis and treatment. She seemed better for a time, but then her father killed her mother and took his own life. That was too much for her to handle."

Dear God. "But you told us our grandparents died in a car accident."

"I didn't want to frighten you. And as for your

mother..." He stared out the window, obviously seeing some painful scene from the past. "I couldn't bear the thought of her taking her own life. When I found the facility in Vermont, it was reputed to be one of the best in the entire world. Your mother thrived there, though she no longer knew me or even that we were married."

"I'm so sorry, Daddy."

He shrugged. "We had eight or nine good years together. They had warned her not to have children, but she was adamant about wanting a family. I've always prayed that none of you would be affected. She continually sabotaged her birth control, and each time she got pregnant, she refused to take the medicines that controlled her mania. By the time you were ten, things had gotten very bad indeed."

"I remember."

"The tipping point was the day I found her playing with knives in the kitchen. She had cut her fingers badly. Swore it was a mistake. But I knew we were nearing the end. Not long after that, she woke up from a dream in the middle of the night and thought I was a burglar trying to strangle her in her sleep."

He stopped and gasped for air, clearly still traumatized after all these years. Shaking his head, he gazed at Mazie bleakly. "I brought doctors here to the house. A dozen of them. They all said the same. The end of her mental competence was coming soon, and if it happened while she was alone with you kids, she might harm you."

"So you sent her away."

"I did. I missed her so badly I thought my heart would break in two. But I had to protect you and your brothers."

Mazie went to him and wrapped her arms around him. "Thank you for telling me."

"I should have done it long before now, but it was so hard to face it…to talk about it."

He was shaking. Mazie felt the lash of guilt for putting him through the retelling, though she was glad to know the truth. "You're a good man. And a good father. I'm so happy you're going with your friends on this trip."

"I'm sorry I won't be here for Christmas."

"No worries," she said blithely. "Gina has asked me to spend the day with her family."

That part was true. He didn't have to know that Mazie had declined the invitation.

She fell into bed that night, but slept only in snatches. Alana and Leila had taken turns answering Mazie's texts. Jane Vaughan had a pulmonary embolism. It was serious…likely a complication from her surgery. But she was being treated with the appropriate medications and would be monitored closely.

Mazie begged both of J.B.'s sisters not to let him know that she was in contact with them.

There was to be no Christmas celebration at the Vaughan homeplace. If Jane stabilized, she might be allowed to leave the hospital for a few hours to celebrate with her family at J.B.'s house, since it was so close to the hospital.

On the twenty-third, Mazie worked all day and then drove her father and brother to the airport. Their flights were only an hour apart, and fortunately in the right order. Jonathan was able to make sure his father got safely on the plane to Fort Lauderdale where he would meet up with his college buddies. Soon after, Jonathan flew out to Arizona.

Hopefully, he would find some relief for the head-aches that plagued him.

That night, Mazie walked the floors in the empty house. She felt like a ghost. A phantom. A woman who wasn't actually real.

The pain had receded for the moment, leaving her pleasantly numb.

She slept on the sofa for five hours. Showered. Went in to work.

Christmas Eve was normally her favorite day of the year. This time, she suffered through it, watching the clock, waiting for the moment she could return home and pull the covers over her head.

Her acting skills were top-notch. When Gina asked once again about Christmas Day, Mazie declined with a smile on her face. Gina assumed—and Mazie didn't correct her—that Mazie was spending the holiday with J.B.

There would be plenty of time later for the pain-ful truth.

All That Glitters closed at four on the twenty-fourth. Mazie handed out beautifully wrapped gifts to all her staff, gave a brief emotional speech and sent everyone on their way.

With the inventory secured and the shop locked up and the alarm set, she headed for home. She had to get through the next thirty-six hours. After that, maybe she could find a way forward. Perhaps she would move to Savannah and open another branch of her popu-lar jewelry shop. That would put her far enough away from J.B.'s orbit not to bump into him, but still close to her family.

Maybe Jonathan could hire someone to help out with their father. Mazie couldn't stay in Charleston any longer. She had to change her life.

The long hours of Christmas Eve were a mockery of all her dreams. As a teenager, she had imagined she would be married by now. With a house of her own, children, a husband. Having a career had been important to her, but no more so than building a future with people she loved. Starting traditions. Sharing special moments.

She sat in front of the TV and watched bits and pieces of movie classics. Funny ones. Sad ones. Hopeful ones.

When that pastime lost its allure, she walked the beach in the dark. From the water's edge, she could look into the windows of large rental houses. Families celebrating. Eating. Laughing.

Never had she felt so alone.

Christmas morning dawned sunny and mild as it so often did in Charleston. As soon as she woke up, all the awful memories came rushing back, not the least of which was the look on J.B.'s face when he exiled her from his mother's hospital room. It had shriveled her soul.

She knew now what she had to do to bring closure to this painful episode of her life. Perhaps she had dreamed the solution in her sleep.

First she showered and dressed for the day. Lycra running pants and a long-sleeve tee would suffice. Then she visited the safe in her father's office.

She riffled through a stack of documents, selected the appropriate one and tucked it in a brown envelope. Next she Googled twenty-four-hour delivery services.

Soon, she would never have to see or speak to J.B. Vaughan ever again.

Eighteen

J.B. was in hell. And operating with a split personality. Thankfully, his mother had recovered to the point that her doctor was comfortable releasing her for a few hours on Christmas Day.

The family had strict instructions to rush her back if certain symptoms occurred.

But Jane Vaughan was glowing. Surrounded by her children and her husband, she was ecstatic to be celebrating the holiday in something other than a hospital gown.

Alana and Leila had thrown together a very creditable feast. Roast turkey with all the fixings. Grandmother Vaughan's sweet potatoes. A few other side dishes, and—procured from a local bakery—a stunning red velvet cake.

Since J.B. didn't own any china—only masculine

earthenware dishes—the womenfolk had opted to break with tradition and use disposable plates to minimize cleanup. J.B.'s drop-in-thrice-a-week housekeeper had been given the week off between Christmas and New Year's to spend with her family.

The meal was outstanding… J.B. felt deep relief and gratitude to see his mother doing so much better. His father was equally exuberant to have his bride back on her feet. Alana and Leila were in a celebratory mood, as well.

The only nagging thorn in J.B.'s soul was Mazie's absence. He had started to call her a dozen times, but he was still so angry that she had revealed their secret to his mother without asking him. In the midst of all the drama, he had actually been convinced that Mazie's mistake caused his mother's relapse.

Later, he realized the truth. He had overreacted.

He owed Mazie an apology for that. But his righteous anger was justified. The secret about their fake engagement hadn't been hers to reveal.

She had gone behind his back. That was why he was angry—right?

Or was he so devastated, because in the midst of everything that had happened, he had finally realized the complete truth. Not only was he heels over ass deep in love with Mazie, he might be willing to believe he had a second chance at forever.

The three recent nights without her in his bed were interminable. He had come to depend on her soft warmth to help him sleep. He worked too hard and had trouble relaxing. Mazie's presence in his life in the midst of his mother's traumatic illness had helped steady him.

Why had she told his mother the engagement was not real? What did she hope to gain?

Her unexpected and dangerous choice felt like a betrayal.

After the midday meal, his parents dozed in the den. J.B. helped clear the table, but his sister shooed him out of the kitchen.

Leila kissed his cheek. "We love you, J.B., but we can do this faster without you. Relax. Check your email. We've got this."

He wandered toward the front of the house, reluctant to go into the den. There were too many memories there. Seeing the beautiful Christmas tree he and Mazie had decorated hurt. He didn't want to remember. He wanted to throw the damned thing out to the curb, ornaments and all.

When the doorbell rang, his heart leaped in shock and momentary hope. But of course it wasn't Mazie. Why would it be? He had sent her away most emphatically.

The barely-twenty-something man standing on the doorstep wore the familiar uniform of a well-known delivery service. He handed J.B. a manila envelope. "Sign here, please."

J.B. scribbled his name on the magnetic screen. "Did you draw the short straw today?"

The young kid shook his head and grinned. "Nope. Jewish. I volunteered. Merry Christmas, sir."

J.B. closed the door and opened the envelope. At first he couldn't process what he was seeing. It was a deed. Not just any deed...but a deed to the building that housed Mazie's jewelry store. And she had signed it over to him.

Leila exited the kitchen, drying her hands on a dishcloth covered with reindeer. "What's that?"

He frowned. "I'm not sure. It seems as if Mazie has finally agreed to let me have her property for my renovation project."

"That's good, isn't it?"

"Yes. But I…"

"But what?"

"I don't know why she's giving it to me now after stonewalling for so long. And why the hell did she tell Mom we weren't engaged without asking me first? The shock could have killed Mom."

"And you're still angry."

"Hell, yes," he said.

Alana gave him a pitying look. "You're such a dope. You don't know Mazie at all. Of course she didn't tell Mom anything. Mom guessed the truth from the very first day you lied to her. She knew you wanted to give her something to cling to before heart surgery."

"She did?"

"Yeah. Mazie kept your secret, J.B. And she kept pretending because Mom asked her to. But you yelled at her and humiliated her in front of all of us and a bunch of nurses and doctors. Bad karma, my brother."

His heart sank. The enormity of his blunder crushed him. "I've got to talk to her," he muttered.

"We're about to open presents," Alana said. "And besides, I don't think you should go rushing over there if you don't have your head on straight. You've hurt

Mazie. You'd better decide what you want from her, or you'll make things even worse."

J.B. made it an hour and a half before he cracked.

He *had* to go talk to Mazie. It couldn't wait. He needed to apologize and tell her he loved her. Or both.

Fortunately, his mother decided she was ready to go back to her hospital bed. The cardiologist had promised that if this next set of tests was acceptable, he would release her on the twenty-seventh.

When the house was finally empty again, J.B. grabbed his keys. He drove across town and on toward the beach, barely even registering the empty streets. His heart pounded in his chest. Would Mazie be willing to talk to him? He had treated her terribly.

When he got to the Tarleton property, the front gates were locked. Fortunately, J.B. had the security codes. Jonathan had given them to him a few months ago when all the family was out of town at the same time. J.B. had checked on the property for them.

Now, he prayed the codes hadn't been changed.

He breathed a sigh of relief when the gates swung open. All the cars were visible, parked in the partially sheltered bays beneath the house. But there was no sign of life anywhere.

Patience.

He took a deep breath, trying to silence his galloping heartbeat. He loped up the front steps, entered a second code and eased open the door.

"Mazie? Jonathan?"

As far as J.B. could tell, no one was home. He walked through the main floor of the house. There was no sign of any activity. No meal. No televisions running. No wrapping paper.

He stopped at the bay window and gazed out at the aquamarine ocean.

And then he saw her. Down by the water's edge, a lone figure, unmistakably feminine, strolled along the shore, bending now and again to pick up a shell.

His body moved instinctively. Exiting the back of the house, he peeled off his socks and shoes, rolled up his pants legs and let himself out of the gate, using the same codes he had memorized earlier.

Mazie had stopped now and was looking toward the horizon, her hands on her hips. The sound of the waves masked his approach.

He stopped a few feet away so as not to scare her.

"Mazie," he called hoarsely.

She spun around, flinching visibly when she saw it was him. "Go away, J.B. This is my beach."

"You can't own beaches in South Carolina," he said. "Please, Mazie. Let me talk to you."

"Didn't you get my package? It's over. You have what you want. Leave me alone."

The scales fell from his eyes. The angel choirs sang. His own stupid brain finally clicked into gear. If he hadn't been such a clueless idiot when he was a younger man, he could have had Mazie by his side and in his bed all these years.

Instead, he'd been saddled with a terrible marriage that had almost destroyed him. He had ended up all alone and had convinced himself that he liked it.

"No," he said soberly. "No, I don't have what I want." He swallowed hard, not quite able to say the words. But he was trying. "I need you, Mazie. I *want* you in my life. I'm sorry I yelled at you and accused you of something you didn't do. I rejected you. Again. Only this time, it was far worse. Alana told me you didn't spill the secret. I should have known better."

She folded her arms around her waist, her posture brittle with *something*. "Apology accepted. And as for the other, I'm no longer interested. Find another woman."

"I can't," he said. "There's only you."

Pain drenched her beautiful eyes. Tears welled in them.

"You don't need to play the game anymore, J.B. I know what you were after. I gave it to you. We're done."

Now he was confused. "Are you talking about the property?"

"Of course," she shouted. "Does any of this sound familiar? *I don't think we have anything to worry about. I've got her eating out of my hand. It won't be a problem.*" She paused to catch her breath. "You didn't want me when I was sixteen, and you don't want me now. You've been *using* me, and I was fool enough to go along with it. But I'm done."

All her anger seemed to winnow away. She stared at him, stone-faced.

He swallowed hard. "You misunderstood," he said carefully.

"Liar."

"I wanted to go out with you when you were sixteen, I swear. I had a huge crush on you. But your brother promised to neuter me if I went through with it because he knew my reputation with girls. So I turned you down. And I've regretted it ever since."

She blinked, her expression wary. "That doesn't excuse the fact that you used sex to coerce me into selling my property to you. I *heard* you, J.B. You can't talk your way out of this one."

His knees felt funny. "I love you, Mazie. I think I have in some way or other my whole life. But I got married, and I screwed that up, and after that, I was too embarrassed to talk to you."

"You don't love me," she whispered. "You *don't*. I heard you on the phone."

God, he had hurt her so badly. He'd tried to protect himself from making another mistake, but in the process, Mazie had become collateral damage.

"I was talking about the mayor," he said. "That was my partner on the phone, yes. But we weren't discussing you. I've been sweet-talking the mayor and the city council into letting us build a city park. They have grant money for beautification. We've offered to go in with them, if they agree, and do the project in tandem."

"The mayor?"

He nodded. "The mayor. Not you. In case you haven't noticed, you've been leading *me* around by the nose, and not the opposite. I adore you, Mazie. I'm sorry it took me so long to admit it, but I'll spend the next six months convincing you if you're interested in a June wedding. Or if we're both scared, we can wait a year. Or two. Or four. But nothing will change on my end. I love you, Mazie Jane."

The sun was hot on the top of his head. He felt dizzy and sick and terrified. Nothing in his life had ever been as important as this. And he had bungled the hell out of it.

"Say it again," she whispered.

"I love you?"

She shook her head. "No. The part where you wanted to take me to the dance when I was sixteen."

His heart lightened. "When you grew up, Mazie— overnight it seemed—it socked me in the stomach. For years you had been this cute, spunky little kid trying to keep up with your brothers and me. Then suddenly you were a princess. I got tongue-tied just trying to talk to you."

"But you let Jonathan get in your head."

"To be fair to your brother, I was kind of a jerk in those days. He was probably right to wave me off."

"I adored you back then," she said, the words wistful.

He tasted fear. "And now?"

She didn't say a word for the longest time. He could almost *feel* the struggle inside her. Finally, she held out her hand. "I love you, Jackson Beauregard Vaughan. I didn't want to, but I do. As embarrassing as it is to admit, I think I loved you way back then and somehow never got over it."

He closed his eyes and inhaled sharply, tilting his face toward the sun, feeling the weight of the world dissipate. Then he smiled at her and dragged her into his arms.

"I think I've been waiting on this moment forever." After kissing her long and thoroughly and reveling in her eager response, he pulled away at last. "Why are you alone on Christmas Day, sweet girl?"

She laid her cheek against his shoulder. "I'm not alone, J.B. I have you. Merry Christmas, my love."

"Merry Christmas, Mazie." He scooped her into his arms. "Is that house behind us really empty?"

She grinned at him, her hair tumbling in the breeze. "Completely. Would you like to join me in my bedroom and open your Christmas present?"

He laughed out loud, startling a trio of seagulls. "Oh, yeah. And just so you know, great minds think alike. I got you the very same thing…"

Epilogue

Jonathan sat in his luxurious Arizona hotel room at the retreat center and read through the packet of meditation techniques that were supposed to diminish his headaches. Nothing seemed to be working. Not expensive pharmaceuticals. Not hippie-dippie mumbo jumbo. With each passing week, he became more fearful that something in his mother's messed-up DNA had triggered a cataclysm in his. A mental meltdown that might change everything about his life.

Or destroy it completely.

The intensity of the headaches scared him more than he wanted to admit. He didn't want to end up like his mother, drugged and helpless in a facility somewhere.

A phone call from his sister had soothed some of his other concerns. Mazie and J.B. were together. With a capital *T.* It boggled the mind, but both of them sounded happy.

He wished them all the best, even if it was a little weird for him personally.

More important, it was a relief to know that whatever happened to him, J.B. was going to make sure Mazie was okay.

At least one member of the Tarleton family would find happiness…

* * * * *

Look for Jonathan's story coming in May 2019!

#2635 THE RANCHER'S BARGAIN

Texas Cattleman's Club: Bachelor Auction
by Joanne Rock

To pay her sister's debt, Lydia Walker agrees to a temporary job as a live-in nanny for hot-as-sin rancher James Harris. There's no denying the magnetic pull between them, but can they untangle their white-hot desire and stubborn differences before time runs out?

#2636 BOMBSHELL FOR THE BOSS

Billionaires and Babies • by Maureen Child

Secretary Sadie Matthews has wanted CEO Ethan Hart for five years—and quitting hasn't changed a thing! But when fate throws him a baby-sized curveball and forces them together again, all the rules are broken and neither can resist temptation any longer...

#2637 THE FORBIDDEN TEXAN

Texas Promises • by Sara Orwig

Despite a century-old family feud, billionaire Texas rancher Jake Ralston hires antiques dealer Emily Kincaid to fulfill a deathbed promise to his friend. But when they're isolated together on his ranch, these enemies' platonic intentions soon become a passion they can't deny...

#2638 THE BILLIONAIRE RENEGADE

Alaskan Oil Barons • by Catherine Mann

Wealthy cowboy Conrad Steele is a known flirt. He's pursued beautiful Felicity Hunt with charm and wit. The spark between them is enough to ignite white-hot desire, but if they're not careful it could burn them both...

#2639 INCONVENIENTLY WED

Marriage at First Sight • by Yvonne Lindsay

Their whirlwind marriage ended quickly, but now both Valentin and Imogene have been matched again—for a blind date at the altar! The passion is still there, but will this second chance mend old wounds, or drive them apart forever?

#2640 AT THE CEO'S PLEASURE

The Stewart Heirs • by Yahrah St. John

Ayden Stewart is a cunningly astute businessman, but ugly family history has him distrustful of love. His gorgeous assistant, Maya Richardson, might be the sole exception—if he can win her back after breaking her heart years ago!

Get 4 FREE REWARDS!

We'll send you 2 FREE Books plus 2 FREE Mystery Gifts.

Harlequin® Desire books feature heroes who have it all: wealth, status, incredible good looks... everything but the right woman.

FREE
Value Over
$20

---

*Ayden Stewart is a cunningly astute businessman,
but ugly family history has him distrustful of love.
His gorgeous assistant, Maya Richardson, might be
the sole exception—if he can win her back after
breaking her heart years ago!*

Read on for a sneak peek of
At the CEO's Pleasure *by Yahrah St. John,
part of her Stewart Heirs series!*

He would never forget the day, ten years ago, when Maya
Richardson had walked through his door looking for a
job. She'd been a godsend, helping Ayden grow Stewart
Investments into the company it was today. Thinking
of her brought a smile to Ayden's face. How could it
not? Not only was she the best assistant he'd ever had,
Maya had fascinated him. Utterly and completely. Maya
had hidden an exceptional figure beneath professional
clothing and kept her hair in a tight bun. But Ayden had
often wondered what it would be like to throw her over
his desk and muss her up. Five years ago, he hadn't gone
quite that far, but he had crossed a boundary.

Maya had been devastated over her breakup with her
boyfriend. She'd come to him for comfort, and, instead,
Ayden had made love to her. Years of wondering what
it would be like to be with Maya had erupted into a

passionate encounter. Their one night together had been so explosive that the next morning Ayden had needed to take a step back to regain his perspective. He'd had to put up his guard; otherwise, he would have hurt her badly. He thought he'd been doing the right thing, but Maya hadn't thought so. In retrospect, Ayden wished he'd never given in to temptation. But he had, and he'd lost a damn good assistant. Maya had quit, and Ayden hadn't seen or heard from her since.

Shaking his head, Ayden strode to his desk and picked up the phone, dialing the recruiter who'd helped him find Carolyn. He wasn't looking forward to this process. It had taken a long time to find and train Carolyn. Before her, Ayden had dealt with several candidates walking into his office thinking they could ensnare him.

No, he had someone else in mind. A hardworking, dedicated professional who could read his mind without him saying a word and who knew how to handle a situation in his absence. Someone who knew about the big client he'd always wanted to capture but never could attain. She also had a penchant for numbers and research like no one he'd ever seen, not even Carolyn.

Ayden knew exactly who he wanted. He just needed to find out where she'd escaped to.

Don't miss what happens next!
At the CEO's Pleasure *by Yahrah St. John,*
part of her Stewart Heirs series!

Available January 2019 wherever
Harlequin® Desire books and ebooks are sold.

www.Harlequin.com

Love Harlequin romance?

DISCOVER.

Be the first to find out about promotions,
news and exclusive content!

 Facebook.com/HarlequinBooks

 Twitter.com/HarlequinBooks

 Instagram.com/HarlequinBooks

 Pinterest.com/HarlequinBooks

ReaderService.com

EXPLORE.

Sign up for the Harlequin e-newsletter and
download a free book from any series at
TryHarlequin.com.

CONNECT.

Join our Harlequin community to share
your thoughts and connect with other
romance readers!
Facebook.com/groups/HarlequinConnection

HARLEQUIN®

**ROMANCE WHEN
YOU NEED IT**

HSOCIAL2018

THE WORLD IS BETTER WITH

Romance

Harlequin has everything from contemporary, passionate and heartwarming to suspenseful and inspirational stories.

Whatever your mood, we have a romance just for you!

Connect with us to find your next great read, special offers and more.

[f] /HarlequinBooks

[🐦] @HarlequinBooks

www.HarlequinBlog.com

www.Harlequin.com/Newsletters

HARLEQUIN®

A *Romance* FOR EVERY MOOD™

www.Harlequin.com

SERIESHALOAD2015